Notes of Deception

Laura Heeger

Dedication

For my children, the loves of my life, and for Pumpkin, my co-pilot.

Acknowledgment

Thanks to my husband, Mike, for encouraging me to fulfill this lifelong dream, reviewing multiple drafts, and his constant love.

Prologue - The Packing List

When I am asked about March 6, 2006, I always start by describing breakfast. Teddy made perfect scrambled eggs with cheese. He said the trick was slow cooking over low heat. Our family of five was in the small kitchen of our Ft. Lauderdale home. The children and I sat in the breakfast nook, and the morning sun spilled through the windows on three sides of us, bathing us in a warm glow.

The wooden, claw-foot table we had inherited from Ted's grandmother just fit the space with a bench for the kids and chairs on each end for Teddy and me. Blue and white curtains with a French country print framed the large windows and skimmed the wooden floors. The '80s white laminate cabinets with brown trim and white Formica countertops were outdated and chipped, but we had grand plans to expand and update the space. We had done a two-story renovation of the house to add a third bedroom and gracious front porch beneath when we bought it, and I knew once we saved again, the next project would be just as beautiful. I adored each and every corner of this home.

Beautiful light flooded all the rooms and it had the interesting character of an older home that had been added onto over the years by the families who had loved it. I sipped my second cup of coffee and poured more juice for the kids while we impatiently awaited the eggs. We chatted and made plans for the day while the eggs bubbled. Once served, we lingered over breakfast together before our day began. After we cleaned up, I got seven-year-old Carter ready for his golf lesson. Ted always took him and practiced his short game while waiting, and I stayed home with the girls, Meryl, just three, and Ruby, five.

When the boys left, the girls and I went into our sunny family room. I sat down to read, and the girls watched cartoons and drew pictures on a long roll of paper drawn out across a child-sized craft table. The room had always been one of my favorites in our home, wrapped in windows and looking over our side yard of green. The floors were rough limestone, and I had the walls painted a Tuscan, sunbaked yellow. The ceiling was peaked and lined in pine, stained the color of honey, which reached down to touch the windows, Cape Cod style. It was always sun-drenched and where the kids and I happily spent most of our days.

Ted's laptop was lying on the couch. When I picked it up to move it, I remembered his request to review a contract for a potential new partner for his consulting business. In a former life, before becoming a stay-at-home mom, I had been a practicing lawyer as an Assistant District Attorney in New York City. Ted had asked me to review the contract and I had been putting it off for far too long. The girls were chattering away in the background, and Sponge Bob was competing aptly in the foreground, as I scrolled through emails looking for the right one until I found one labeled "Packing List." I paused because we had plans to go with his business partner and his wife to Las Vegas in several weeks, and I asked Ted to send me some ideas about what I should pack. Procrastinating from the task at hand, I clicked the email open and found a long list that was clearly not meant for me. It included negligees, the "mix CD I made for you," bathing suits, sex toys, and other items I couldn't process.

It was signed, "I love you sooooo much, Teddy."

I finally looked at the "to" line and saw the address "babettehaveit." I didn't know who that was, but it was not me, Maggie Melody. I ran to the bathroom and threw up. Gripping the toilet, my legs buckled to the turquoise tile floor as my world spun away from me.

Teddy was, I thought, the love of my life, my soulmate. I was certain, I thought, of the man I knew to be my husband. I called my parents, who were visiting my brother, Judd, and his newborn son in Chicago, to ask for their help. In those first hours, my brother asked if the woman Ted was seeing was a stripper. I was shocked by his question, but Judd haltingly explained that Ted had made small comments throughout the years about the lifestyle he lived as a traveling business consultant, which Judd had dismissed as bravado at the time, but which concerned him now.

When Ted returned later that day, and after I had sent the children to be with his mother so "we could discuss some things," I confronted him with Judd's suspicion as part of the bigger conversation, asking, "Is she a stripper?"

Instead of answering, Ted countered, "Why would you say that?"

And I knew.

It hit me like a punch to the stomach and knocked the air out of me. I gasped for breath as I remembered the one other time he had used that exact question with me. It had been almost nine months earlier, the previous July, about a month before my 35th birthday, Ted said he loved me so much he couldn't wait any longer to give me my birthday present. He pulled out an unwrapped box of sapphire and diamond earrings and a matching necklace. I was shocked at the extravagance and amused by the thought of an Oprah Winfrey show I had seen just that week. Oprah had discussed a book called *The Script*. The book describes a husband who cheats, and says that he will buy extravagant gifts and give them to his wife at odd times.

When I opened Ted's gift, that commentary popped into my mind, and I jokingly asked, "Are you cheating on me or something?"

Ted smiled and, with a tilt of his head, slowly asked, "Why would you say that?"

At the time, I explained and apologized to him, laughing at the absurdity of the thought.

On March 6, 2006, the memory of that gift and his question to me came back like a punch to the gut. I knew when he repeated that question that my husband's affair was not with another housewife or a doctor in one of the hospitals he consulted for - it was with a stripper.

Maybe that's why I always remember the scrambled eggs for breakfast on that day, my kitchen with sunlight spilling through the windows, lighting my children's faces, and the sunbaked walls of our family room with my girls coloring in the corner. Maybe those memories swaddled the others to allow my mind to survive what was to come.

***

Fifteen years later, as I packed up my beloved home, memories of that horrible day still clung to the corners of each room. I stayed in the home to provide stability for my three young children and for me. I fought for it because I didn't want to let Ted and Amber, the other woman, drive me from the home I had created to raise my family.

I filed for divorce on St. Patrick's Day, eleven days after I read that "Packing List" email. In that short time, I rushed us into counseling to try and save our marriage. The therapist said Ted needed to call Amber on speaker phone and break up with her to begin to restore the trust between us. Ted had demurred, asking if he could have a long weekend with Amber to say goodbye first.

I said no.

Following a week of intense counseling sessions, the therapist turned to me and said, "Ted is a sociopath, which is a personality disorder. He is not capable of loving you, and that will not change."

Dumbfounded, I stammered, "Does that mean I have to get a divorce?"

Her startling reply was simply, "Yes."

Teddy had sat between us throughout the exchange without uttering a single word. Looking back, perhaps it was a relief to him that he didn't have to hide his true self anymore. For me and my kids, however, experiencing his real identity was confusing, hurtful, and at times terrifying.

We separated immediately and divorced about a year later. I thought leaving him was the hardest decision I would make - it wasn't. It was far harder to hold to that decision as a single mother of three young children as I began to try and raise them alone without enough money to pay our bills. I ran up credit card debt to pay their tuition at our local church. One year, I sold some of my jewelry to buy their Christmas gifts. I worried endlessly as I juggled transitioning from a stay-at-home mom to a junior lawyer at a boutique law firm. The firm graciously understood my sometimes-erratic schedule when one of the kids got sick, or I had to be in court for my divorce.

The thing I never anticipated, even with all I had learned about Ted in those few short months since I had discovered his secret life and his psychology, was that he would fight me in court for years beyond the divorce. Ted not only fought not to support me after twelve years of marriage but also fought not to support his own children. To my astonishment, the courts and justice system that I had believed in so heartily in the beginning largely bent to his will. How I didn't see his personality disorder during my marriage has haunted me. Once I was aware of who Ted really was, he reveled in it and drew out the game of our divorce, as he saw it, with glee.

I had never known anyone who had been divorced and didn't know you could even have a divorce trial - until I had one. It was three weeks full of salacious details about Ted's secret life with Amber, which, to my horror, attracted spectators in the Ft. Lauderdale courthouse. Lawyers, forensic accountants, and private investigators became a daily part of my life as file boxes filled with binders brimming with thousands of pages of depositions, tax returns, credit card statements, bank records, and finally, transcripts. Strangers gawked as my life fell apart. By the time we went to trial, I thought I knew all the terrible things he had done. I was wrong.

He was a business consultant, which involved constant traveling and enabled him to lead a double life. I found out that he had frequented strip clubs, spending huge amounts of money we did not have. As the co-owner of a small consulting firm, his double life was financed primarily through his company credit card, which enabled him to hide it all from me. What Ted hadn't counted on was his office manager, Liz. As we prepared for the trial, I remembered her sudden firing the previous December and called her.

She answered the phone, saying, "I assumed the call I would get about Ted would be from the FBI. I'm relieved it's from you."

Liz agreed to meet me for lunch at a cafe on trendy Las Olas Boulevard in downtown Ft. Lauderdale. Given her comment on the phone, I was terrified of what I would discover from her. As I dressed for the lunch, it all felt unreal, almost like I was living in a spy movie. We had agreed to meet in a public space where both of us would feel safe.

I found her sitting outside on the patio, sipping a seltzer. She stood to greet me, and after we said hello and hugged each other in solidarity, we sat. Polite small talk seemed bizarre given the circumstances, and so we ordered quickly when the server appeared. Once alone again, Liz passed an envelope of paperwork across the table to me.

"I've kept copies because I'm frightened that I could be implicated in all of this," she explained.

"What is all of this?" I asked, truly perplexed.

"Proof of what he was doing. Like I said, I keep waiting for the FBI to call." She said, pushing her hair back from her face.

"I really don't think I understand what was going on or the extent of it," I admitted.

"It's all about money. Just follow the money. These documents give you what you need to take care of yourself and the kids in the divorce. I'm so sorry you got caught in this."

I offered a half-smile. "I don't know how to thank you, Liz. I still just can't believe any of this is really happening, and I'm embarrassed that I didn't see it."

"Don't be. He fooled everyone. Even his partner in the business, Dwayne. Ted said he'd handle the money, and Dwayne was blindly trusting. I think he was just glad he didn't have to do the books. By the end, Ted was handling all the company finances and had even locked me, the office manager, out of QuickBooks. He worked every angle and even took a free apartment from one hospital in Ohio instead of full pay. I only knew because he had me arrange it all. During all these other shenanigans, the business-backed Dwayne's buys into high-stakes poker games. I doubt his wife knew about that little arrangement. I'm sure Ted figured that if his overspending and theft ever came out, Dwayne couldn't go after him, given all the gambling. There's no way Dwayne knew how much Ted was taking out of the company, though. By the end, it was Ted's personal ATM."

"You figured all of this out? Is that why he fired you?"

"Sort of. But he doesn't know how much I know. I saw his spending on the corporate card. I guess you know the kinds of places. But the amounts were crazy, and I was worried he would drive us out of business. I didn't know what to do so I wrote to *Dear Amy* for advice."

"Dear Amy? The advice columnist?"

"Yeah. I really didn't know what to do. She told me to confront him with evidence, assuming he would come to his senses and stop for the good of the company. I was scared to directly confront Ted, so instead, I put together a spreadsheet of the spending on strip clubs and gave it to Dwayne."

"I guess I know how that turned out." I shook my head with shame for what my husband had done.

"Yeah, but not right away. I wasn't fired for a couple of months, and then they told me they had lost confidence in me."

"I'm so sorry, Liz. I'm horrified at all that Ted has put you through. I don't know how to apologize for his behavior enough."

"Not your mess to clean up. Your husband is a real jackass if you'll excuse my language. If this information can help you and the kids, I'm glad. This whole thing stinks to high heaven."

She reached across the table and briefly squeezed my hand.

We finished lunch, trying to make conversation and studiously ignoring the file folder still on the table with us. I pushed my food around on my plate until Liz signaled that she was done. Finally, I paid, and we hugged, holding onto each other briefly.

"You stay in touch now, you hear? And take good care of those babies of yours; they'll need you now more than ever," she said, a tear in her eye.

"I will," I said, blinking back my own tears.

When I got home, I relieved the babysitter for Meryl and then checked on her as she napped. Her big, loopy curls lay on her pillow as she clung to the pink floral blanket that I had swaddled her in as a baby. For the thousandth time, I prayed this wasn't all happening and then pulled her bedroom door shut again. In the kitchen, my hands shook as I opened the envelope. Copies of checks made out to Ted for tens of thousands of dollars, credit card statements, receipts, the strip club spending spreadsheet Liz mentioned, and copies of emails all fell onto my kitchen table. The last paper to drop from the file was a photocopy of a newspaper advice column dated January 6, 2005. Through a thick, hot blur of tears, I leafed through the pile and then called my lawyer.

The revelations of all those photocopies hit hard. Beyond the emotional upheaval, I was forced to file for Innocent Spouse Protection from the IRS. I had never heard of the protection before, but it turns out I had unknowingly co-signed falsified tax returns based on the information Liz had provided. My lawyer and the forensic accountants told me the IRS status would protect me from being prosecuted, and we provided evidence collected in preparation for trial, including select copies of the paperwork from Liz, to prove the defense to the government. We waited months for the IRS response, and when it came, relief rolled over me in a tidal wave. I also worried about the blowback that would come from Ted, as my filing for protection would also have tipped them off to his financial shenanigans if they hadn't previously been aware. I learned later that they had come after him for hundreds of thousands of dollars in unpaid taxes, but I never knew if it was my filing that had triggered their interest.

Our divorce trial began in the spring of 2007. I learned that Amber was a stripper living in a weekly motel outside Dallas when they met. The checks he wrote to himself from his firm helped cover her expenses and an apartment they referred to as "the nest." He used our savings to put her through an aesthetician school. Private investigators found evidence of a lifestyle I couldn't recognize. It included: a citation for sex in a public park; receipts for jewelry he bought in pairs for both Amber and me; high-priced vacations they took that he had me plan under the ruse that I was planning work events for clients; and even airfare to have Amber visit him in our home in Ft. Lauderdale when I was out of town visiting my parents, while three-year-old Meryl was home with them.

As the trial churned on, I pulled myself out of bed each morning and had to force myself to chew and swallow food at each meal. I joked with my friends that divorce was the best diet on the planet as the pregnancy weight I had carried since Meryl was born now fell off of me. I was on leave from work but still had to drive carpool, host play dates, read stories, help with homework, and wait for my children to fall asleep every night so I could weep.

At times, the horror of the revelation that nothing in my life had been real was too much to process. There is a thick book by Wally Lamb titled *I Know This Much Is True*, which I had purchased just before everything happened and which continued to lay, unopened, on my nightstand. I remember reading the title over and over and wondering if I would ever know what in my life had been true. To this day, I have never read Lamb's book beyond the title but have kept it, perhaps as a reminder.

I became depressed and began to have anxiety attacks. My doctor prescribed medication for the depression, which helped, as well as for the anxiety. He tested me for STDs and HIV, and his nurse held me as I wept during the blood draws in fear and disbelief at what my husband had exposed me to. I found counseling, too, that allowed me to cry and process away from the worried gazes of my children.

Even today, I still struggle, at times, with the hollowness that remains. I've learned to grow around the gaps of understanding like tree roots around a sidewalk trying to survive. Whatever Ted was in reality, I had believed he was the love of my life and a good man. I was wrong on both counts.

The trial ended, and we were divorced in May 2007. Ted kept me in court for eight more years, fighting over child support and alimony. At one of our hearings, an elderly statesman of a judge leaned over the bench and chastised us for not being able to resolve our issues and suggested we use his chambers to "talk it out." He then recessed court for thirty minutes and ushered Ted and me, alone, into his offices just off the courtroom.

While sitting across the judge's large conference table from me, Ted smirked and said, "What he doesn't understand is that I will always be able to lie better than you can ever tell the truth."

We sat in silence for the next twenty-nine minutes until we were called back into the courtroom.

***

The weekend I discovered Ted's deception, I went for a run, and the song "Unwritten" by Natasha Bedingfield played. She sang,

"Feel the rain on your skin; no one else can feel it for you. Only you can let it in."

At that moment, the Ft. Lauderdale sky opened and drops from the regular summer afternoon thunderstorm fell.

"No one else, no one else, can speak the words on your lips, drench yourself in words unspoken, live your life with arms wide open; today is where your book begins; the rest is still unwritten."

As the song played, the rain beat against my face, and I stopped running and looked up. At that moment, it felt like the universe was speaking to me and telling me it would all be alright. Today, almost exactly fifteen years later, I feel like I am finally turning the page on a very dark chapter in my life and beginning to write my own story again. As Meryl, my youngest, is off to college, I am ready to reclaim my narrative.

❖

Chapter 1 - My New Chapter

The sun shone as I drove onto the pea-gravel driveway of the New England farmhouse I had bought after a whirlwind house-hunting trip three months ago. I found an associate professor role in Criminology at Eastern Connecticut University and a lovely, small house in a waterfront village, Bell Harbor. I had always been a gardener in Florida and would need to take back this yard, which, although small, had been sorely neglected. I sat in the car and admired the white clapboard house, its cupola with tiny stained-glass windows, and its oddly pitched roof. The wrap-around porch held a deep swing with plenty of room left for a small table and two or three chairs. The three bedrooms inside would let my kids visit and hopefully even welcome grandkids one day. The house was old, from the 1890s, and needed work, but that meant I could afford it and the view that it came with. The generous porch overlooked Bell Harbor and the Connecticut River beyond as it wound its way south to Long Island Sound. I let Pumpkin, my yellow Labrador rescue, out to mark her new territory, and then we both stretched and climbed the broad front steps into our new home.

The moving van arrived at lunchtime two days later, and I quickly unpacked the boxes they had brought, adding to all those I had driven up with myself. I decided some memories would not be a part of this home, so I hauled eight heavy file boxes of divorce paperwork up to the attic. I decided they could sit there and collect dust until I could scan them and then, finally, throw them away. I walked through the house, now filled. The cupola which was boarded up when I arrived, was now exposed. It sat over the tiny entry hall, and streams of light cast down from the colorful stained-glass windows on its four sides. A wide living room welcomed you into the home with a broad fireplace centered on the long wall.

The dining room opened opposite the fireplace with the kitchen behind it. The main bedroom was clustered with the others in the back of the house and featured beautiful afternoon light through windows on two walls. The original oak floors that helped sell me on the home ran through all of the bedrooms, and my scrubbing over the last few days had left them gleaming. I carried the leftover furniture I still wanted to keep, boxes of memorabilia for longer-term storage, Christmas and Easter decorations, and some other odds and ends into what would be the office until I could move them all into a storage space.

I poured myself a glass of white wine, walked out to the porch, and sat on my swing as the sun set. Pumpkin put her head on my lap and then made her way onto the swing next to me. I gazed down over the sleepy village of Bell Harbor. Would this town give me the fresh start I was looking for? The beauty of the town lights, reflected off the river beyond, reminded me to be grateful and stop worrying. I scratched behind Pumpkin's ear, her favorite spot.

"Tomorrow, we have to take back the yard, girl."

Pumpkin sighed in agreement without opening her eyes. We had a lot of work to do.

I am up early, usually around five. So, by the time the sun rose that Monday, I had already had my coffee, was dressed, and was ready to go. I had learned in Florida the dangers the sun could pose to my freckled, Scottish skin, so I pulled on my wide-brimmed hat and tucked in my red, wavy hair to keep it out of the way. I then coaxed Pumpkin out of her bed and into the overgrown yard. I laid down a moving blanket as a makeshift bed for her and went to get my still-packed box of gardening tools, clippers, rake, and a box of lawn & leaf bags I had picked up at the grocery store. After laying out my tools on the dewy grass next to the sleeping Pumpkin, I surveyed my task. From a bird's view the yard was square with the house in the southeast corner. There was a hedge running around the perimeter, which appeared to be mostly hydrangea, and there were sorely neglected flower beds around the front porch, which wrapped the front and east sides of the home. The house sat up on Nutmeg Hill, which provided a view of the village of Bell Harbor and the water beyond.

I put on my garden gloves, picked up my large pruning clippers, and got to work on the hedge. After an hour of trimming it back and raking up the debris, I could see not only a little more of the grass of my front yard but a neighbor peddling an ancient-looking bicycle towards me while balancing a full glass.

"You're smart to be at it so early before it gets more humid," she said with a smile. "I'm sorry I didn't get over here when you first moved in. I was away over the weekend and just got back last night. I'm Megan Jeremy, and I live just down the hill. I brought you some iced tea."

"How sweet of you, thank you. I'm Maggie Glass," I said, walking around the hedge and out the battered front gate to shake her hand and take the cup.

After a large swallow, I added, "Refreshing, thanks. It's great to meet you. Have you lived around here long?"

"My husband and I moved here when he took a teaching position at Eastern Connecticut - that was twenty years ago. He passed away five years ago, but I stayed on because it's such a great little village."

"I'm so sorry about your husband."

"Thank you. It was cancer and very quick. Looking back, maybe that was a blessing. But enough about me, what brings you to our little village?"

"I start as an associate professor at Eastern Connecticut in a couple of weeks. All my kids are up and out now, and this is a fresh start for me. It's been me and the kids for so long that I want to try being just Maggie for a while."

"Well, this is the place to do it. This village has always been wonderful to me. I own the coffee shop in town now, Grounded. I bought it about a year after I lost Bill. I have a great manager for the store, although most days I go in - which is why I'm up early and on my way in now."

"Oh! I don't want to keep you then. It was wonderful to meet you, Megan, and so kind of you to stop by. I'd love to offer you a glass of wine on my porch to say thank you."

"Terrific, I'll count on it. Just knock on my door. I'm the blue house, white trim," she said while pointing behind her and then peddled off.

Four hours later, the hedge was tamed. Five bags of clippings were stacked at the curb for collection, and Pumpkin and I made our way inside for a well-earned bath, a chicken salad sandwich for me, a dog treat, and fresh water for her.

That afternoon, I found a storage space not too far away and began ferrying the contents I had stored temporarily in my office. As the locker filled, my house began to feel less cluttered and more like a home, and I was able to set up the third bedroom as a proper workspace for myself. The room faced east and captured the lovely morning sun. My kids had joked with me for years about my tendency to throw things away prematurely. I thought this storage locker proved them wrong, as I filled it with memories of our lives together. The task went on into the next day until my Stor-It-All space was neatly packed, and my house was left with only what I loved and needed.

I spent the rest of the week unpacking and arranging my bedroom, kitchen, and guest room until I felt both settled and restless in the home. Friday after lunch, I leashed Pumpkin, and we walked down Nutmeg Hill to explore the village on foot. The afternoon sky boasted bright sun and low, fluffy clouds that looked like cotton balls floating above the river. At one end of the harbor town was a park along the river, with dense clumps of trees at one end, but then it opened up to the town green and the shops along Water Street. It was the main route through town and offered all I would need: the local co-op for groceries; a ladies' store that leaned preppy; Megan's charming coffee shop, Grounded; a lovely little bookstore heavy on mysteries and Connecticut lore, the Book Cellar; a kitchen gadget store; a small but well-stocked hardware store; a men's store that was very tweedy;

a boulangerie with Parisian style bread; a few restaurants; and a realtor. The fact that I could walk to them all in just 10 minutes was the icing on top. I tied Pumpkin's leash to a lamp post and ran into the co-op, joining and picking up staples and a couple of treats for the week. Pumpkin and I then ambled down Water Street to Grounded, admiring the river, which peeked between the buildings along the way. I went in to say hello to Megan and treat myself to an iced chai latte.

"Hey, Maggie!" she sang out from behind the counter as I walked in. "How's unpacking going?"

I couldn't help but smile as I looked at her. She had her mane of brown curly hair stacked up on her head and wound into a bright red handkerchief, and her green eyes sparkled as she welcomed me to her shop. The cafe had a long rectangular counter against the back wall with a glass front and a grouping of small, round tables along the windows in front. Beadboard lined the walls and was painted a deep blue, echoing the water across the road. The white tables and chairs contrasted the walls and dark wood floors. The whole place seemed warm and welcoming, much like its owner.

"It's just about done, actually. I like to get it over with and get settled. So, Pumpkin and I are out exploring the village."

"You're a better woman than me. I think I still have boxes in the attic from when Bill and I moved in that I haven't gotten to," she said with a shrug and a smile.

"We stopped in for an iced chai latte because I just picked up some snacks at the co-op. Are you free later to drop by for a nibble and a glass of wine?" I asked. "I'll return your clean glass, too."

"Sounds great. I leave here around five because Natalie is closing tonight."

She nodded towards her assistant, who was pouring my latte into a to-go cup.

"Terrific, see you around six?" I said as I paid Natalie and stabbed a straw into my cup.

"See you then, thanks, Maggie." She snuck me a treat for Pumpkin on my way out the door.

❖

Chapter 2 - Megan

Megan arrived just as I was bringing out a tray of cheese, crackers, and grapes to add to the wine I had already set out. Although the porch looked east, sunsets cast a rose-colored light on the village buildings and harbor beyond that had a magical quality.

"It's beautiful, isn't it?" I said as I noticed her taking in the view.

"You won't tire of it. No matter what life has brought me, this view reminds me that there is still beauty in the world," Megan said as she scooted back onto the swing. "I get this view off my back porch. Next time, we'll meet there, and I'll show you."

"Sounds great," I said as I poured us each a glass of wine and served up two small plates of nibbles.

We talked late into the night about Bill and his cancer and her struggles to find her footing after her loss. She spoke of learning to navigate the loneliness and of finally buying the coffee shop business and how it had helped bring her out of her grief. I spoke of my children and the ordeal of managing their father and all the trauma he had caused. I shared my disbelief at having loved him for so long, not seeing who and what he was, and the loss of trust it had caused - both in others and myself.

"I tried to save the marriage when I first discovered his affair. We went to couples counseling, but I ended up finding out he was a sociopath and that I really just needed a divorce."

"How awful, I'm so sorry. You hear about situations like that but never think they're real." She reached over and squeezed my hand. "I was lucky to have found Bill. It's why I'm not so keen on dating – there'll never be another like him. Maybe one love is all each of us get," reflected Megan, as she took a sip of her wine.

"I refuse to believe that. I have to think someone else is out there for me and for you, too. With all that happened with Ted, I worked hard to learn to trust again and believe in love. I don't know if I can ever really understand him, but I got glimpses of who he really was, unfortunately, over time. Once the therapist declared him a sociopath, it was as if a mask he had worn during our relationship fell away. He was cruel to me, but the worst thing was that he was cruel to our kids. He would use them to hurt and manipulate me, but they were often emotionally hurt in the process. It was gut-wrenching as their mother, and there was almost nothing I could do to protect them from him."

"Couldn't the courts do anything? Couldn't he lose visitation?"

"Not unless I was willing to bring my children into the loud, chaotic New York City family court and have them testify against their father. They would be subject to cross-examination by his lawyer, who was an absolute bottom feeder. I constantly wrestled with that choice, but their therapist and my lawyer agreed we likely didn't have enough to have the courts keep him away from them. It was a no-win situation. As much as I tried to protect my kids, the family courts continued to allow visitation twice a month, and so, for the last 15 years, I have tried to manage him while shielding them. My family would say, 'This will all catch up with him,' but so far, it hasn't."

"I'm so sorry, Maggie. It's scary that he could have behaved one way with you for so long while this other person lived inside him."

"That's why I'm so proud of my kids and who they have grown up to be - despite their father. And that's why, once Meryl left for college, I moved up here to claim a new life for myself. I don't want to be someone who spends her life looking backward. He's taken enough from me already."

"Bill and I never had children. We always thought we'd have time for that later," she said, trailing off.

"I'm so sorry, Megan." This time, I reached over to hold her hand.

She smiled, saying, "Don't get me wrong. I don't regret a day with Bill. Your story makes me realize all over again how lucky we were. I haven't really moved on in that department since I lost him. Not for reasons like yours, but because I don't think I can match what we had. How do I replicate that?"

"I'm certainly no expert on love, but I don't think you can. Whatever you find next won't compete with what you and Bill had. It'll be unique and new. You deserve love again, Megan, and so do I." We clinked glasses and toasted to the love that we hoped was waiting for each of us.

"Are you excited to teach?" she asked, not so subtly changing the subject.

"Excited, nervous, all kinds of emotions. I've always wanted to teach and hope I can make a difference for the students. I've spent all summer planning the course and developing case studies, which I hope will be more interactive than a normal university lecture."

"You're in criminology, right? Forgive my ignorance, but what exactly is that?"

"Good question. Criminology is the study of crime and criminal behavior. We pull from many other fields to inform our study, including sociology, psychology, economics, statistics, and anthropology."

"Do you have a degree in criminology?"

"No, actually. I have economics and law degrees and practiced criminal law both as a prosecutor and then as a defense attorney for many years. The university was looking for a more practical application of criminology, and so I qualified. And I'm thrilled."

"Well, it all sounds very *Criminal Minds*. I love that show. Will you study real crimes?"

"Yes, and fictional ones I've developed as case studies. I'm hoping we can look at the development of law enforcement over the years as the criminal element has also adapted."

"Sounds fascinating."

"You're welcome to audit any class you'd like. It'd be nice to have a friendly face in the room."

"Oh, I'd stick out like a sore thumb with all those kids."

We both laughed, as I repeated my invitation to join us.

We talked for hours and by midnight, we were fast friends, having laughed and cried over a shared understanding of loss, grief, and hope for a fresh start for each of us in Bell Harbor. After Megan left, I tidied the porch and got quickly to bed, as the next day, I planned another full day of yard work. This was my last weekend before I began my new job, and I hoped to clean up and plant the beds around the porch.

❖

25

Chapter 3 - The Post

Monday morning, I was up early as the first rays of sun broke through the clear sky. I dressed, and Pumpkin and I walked around the block while I sipped my second cup of coffee from a travel mug. Today was my first day at Eastern Connecticut.

The nameplate on the door, Assoc. Professor Glass still made me think of my father. He was a professor for much of his career at Columbia Medical School and was the only Professor Glass I had ever known. I took back my maiden name with the new job and was still adjusting to no longer being a Melody as my children were. I leaned the bag carrying my diplomas and a picture of my children against the file cabinet and surveyed the cozy office. It had a gray patterned carpet, with a worn, dark wood desk facing the door and a large window behind. There were matching low file drawers to the right as you entered and a chair opposite the desk for visitors, which left just enough room for a coat rack in the back corner to the left of the window. I immediately decided the small office needed a plant and began to unpack what little belongings I had brought with me.

"Knock, knock! I'm Jim Raven, Sociology. Welcome, Professor Glass," said a smiling man as he entered my office.

He had dark curly hair with gray at the temples, dark brown eyes with a ruddy complexion, and a full-toothed smile. He towered over me with a long, lean frame as he held out his hand of welcome.

We shook hands as I said, "Maggie, please. It's great to meet you."

"Ready for your first day?"

"I hope so. I'm excited to meet my students."

"Well, let me give you the nickel tour and then deposit you at your classroom. We can grab coffee on the way."

"Terrific, let me grab my bag."

We walked along a path that wound through the brick buildings as Jim pointed out key features, including the cafeteria and even some shortcuts. Thirty minutes later, I had a rudimentary understanding of the layout of the campus, a slightly better grasp of the buildings I would need to navigate regularly, and a large cup of coffee perched on the lectern I would use shortly.

"Thanks for the whirlwind tour. You're quite the welcome wagon," I said with a warm smile.

"Happy to oblige. I had someone do the same for me when I began ten years ago, and it made all the difference, so now I pay it forward. A group of us gather Fridays for lunch if you're around - we meet at the Blue Dog Cafe at one o'clock – and all are welcome."

"Count me in - sounds like a great way to meet folks. Again, thank you so much for the tour."

"You're very welcome. Good luck today," he said with a slight bow and wave of his hand.

Just as he left, the students began to file in. After everyone was seated, I began.

"Welcome to Criminology 101. I'm Associate Professor Maggie Glass. I'm a lawyer, and I was a prosecutor in New York City for five years before having children. I then went into private practice as a criminal defense attorney in Florida for the last 15 years. Together, this semester, we will explore the criminal mind and how the authorities have grappled with crime over time. Any questions before we get started?"

Hands shot up across the room. I grabbed my coffee, walked around in front of the lectern, leaned back against it, and began to engage with the class. By the end of our hour together, I had learned at least some of the names of the 24 students and was clear on the need for some more current examples for them. I would need to dig through the news to find examples of crimes to which they could better relate. Hopefully, the updated content would provide more context to the historical examples I had already planned.

Later that night, with Pumpkin curled at my feet on the couch and a glass of white wine, I began to research modern-day policing techniques comparable to those I had used in class. An alert popped up on my screen that my daughter, Ruby, had posted on Instagram, so I toggled over to take a break. She had posted on her stepmother's page. I paused, taking a deep breath before I read what she was reacting to with an emoji heart. Her stepmother, Amber, was the woman who so long ago had caused me so much pain, and I knew that reading any further would only open feelings I didn't want. I swallowed hard and read the post anyway.

It read:

> *As Ted and I prepare for our trip to Paris and the Maldives, I just can't believe that I didn't document our last journey there in 2011. We are so very lucky to*

be celebrating 18 years together since we met on Labor Day. I'm just so crazy in #love with this empowering man! He brings out the very best in everything I do!

This little girl looks forward to the next 18 years!

#thisisit #lovebirds

I read it again. 18 years? That was longer than I had thought they had been together. Tears pooled in my eyes, and I wiped them away with the back of my hand and read it again. I was surprised by the pain and the tears so many years later. I chastised myself for believing I had finally known the real extent of my ex's deception. In the back of my mind, I had always suspected the truth was worse than I knew, but it still managed to take my breath away. I calculated what I was doing 18 years ago and what I believed the state of my marriage to be back then. I was pregnant with Meryl and believed myself married to the love of my life. I allowed the tears to spill over and roll down my cheeks as I mourned for what felt like the thousandth time.

I dragged myself up off the couch, splashed water on my face, and, knowing it was a bad idea, sat back down to post a response.

I wrote:

@AMelody - 18 years ago, on Labor Day, Ted was married to me, and you were a stripper at the Brass Ass just outside Dallas. Yours is not a story about #lovebirds but a story about a #cheater and an #adulterer. I still have copies of the divorce depositions you both gave for the trial, laying the

> *sordid facts all out in nauseating detail, plus the receipts for how much you cost us…. Have some respect for the family you destroyed in the process.*

The hurt of having one of my own children "heart" Amber's post, even if Ruby wasn't calculating the years involved as I was, poured into those few very public sentences I wrote. I had never confronted Amber. Not once during all the depositions or the trial. I had been swallowing back my pain for the sake of the kids for fifteen years, and for some reason, this dumb, hashtag filled post was just too much to ignore. Was I supposed to act as if it was all okay? As if all they had done was acceptable? Maybe posting was petty and childish, but I couldn't help myself. I closed my iPad and went to bed.

I woke the next morning feeling better and getting text messages from my children brimming with their personalities. Carter's text was full of concern about why I was even reading Amber's Instagram page and putting myself through that pain again. Ruby's message was apologetic but fearful of alienating her stepmother and father if she retracted her "heart." Meryl's text told of the flash of anger by her stepmother and her father while still asking how I was doing and if I wanted to talk. I replied, thanking all of them and telling them I was okay, I loved them, and that we would chat later in the week. I decided I would call them over the weekend when I could linger and talk.

Friday morning flew by as I was excited about lunch at the Blue Dog Cafe and the chance to meet more colleagues and neighbors. I arrived just at one and saw Jim sitting at a long table with six or seven others. My nervousness was relieved when I saw Megan at one end of the table, deep in conversation. She was talking with a woman who was slightly older than us and very animated in her responses.

As I approached, Jim rose, announcing, "Hey everybody, this is Maggie Glass, new to the university and to Bell Harbor. Maggie, this is everybody."

He waved his hand across the table as a magician might when completing a trick and then sat back down.

"Grab a seat. We haven't ordered. If you haven't eaten here yet, you can't go wrong. Half a sandwich and the soup of the day is very popular," he added with a wink.

I thanked him and grabbed an empty seat diagonally across from Megan, the last open chair at the table. After we ordered and got our food, everyone took turns introducing themselves and explaining their relation to the group. Most were university-affiliated except for Megan and the woman she had been speaking to as I arrived, Sarah Cooper. Sarah owned the bakery in town, a French-style boulangerie, and everyone at the table agreed that she made the best bread I would ever taste. She blushed at the compliments, shaking her head. She was pleasantly plump, as my mother would say, reflecting a love of the carbohydrates she baked. Her skin was almost translucent against the dark hair piled on her head. Speckles of flour dusted across her shirt, betraying her bakers' hours, which I supposed were already over for the day. She exuded warmth, and I was drawn to her immediately.

The conversation flowed, and I heard about upcoming county fairs in the area and apple-picking trips being planned. There was a little talk about the university administration and changes to class schedules for next semester, but it was brief to be sure not to exclude those who weren't at the school. I noticed Jim eyeing Megan a couple of times and made a mental note to ask her about it later. I listened more than I talked throughout the meal, learning about those around me and the new town I intended to make my home. Afterward, I headed back to Pumpkin and the house cleaning I had put off all week.

That evening, just as I was clearing my dinner dish to the sink, FaceTime rang, and it was Carter. I settled in to chat and immediately saw concern on his face.

After our normal catch-up, he launched into the reason for his call.

"Mom, Dad's angry about what you posted."

"I don't understand. It's not a revelation. It's the truth."

"Amber and Dad are starting a new business, a line of skin creams and some other things Dad is working on - remember she's an aesthetician? Well, they have a financial backer, and he saw your post and the part about her being a stripper. They almost lost the deal."

"I still don't understand. She was a stripper. It's a fact. She can't re-write history."

"She says you're lying and that it's not true. She says she was a model."

"What? She and your dad testified to how they met in their depositions and at the divorce trial. He went to a strip club where she worked. I have copies of the transcripts."

"I know - you don't have to convince me. I lived through it with you."

"You know, I kept all those transcripts because, in the back of my mind, I think I knew someday your dad would distort the facts of what actually happened."

"You don't need it for me, Mom, or the girls. We know the truth. Leave it in your storage locker, collecting dust. All it can do is cause pain."

"So, what should I do?"

"Nothing. Amber took down your post."

"Can she do that? Take down my post?"

"Yeah, she can. And she blocked you from posting again on her page."

"And I'm supposed to be okay with her proclaiming to the world how long they've been together?"

"Mom, it's been 15 years since you divorced."

"It's not that – it's the lack of respect for our marriage … our family … then and now. They have no shame about what they did and no remorse for all the pain they have caused. We - you, me, and your sisters - our family deserves better."

"I get it. I'm sorry you're so hurt, Mom. Are you okay?"

"I am, thanks, Carter. I love you. I think just posting that, standing up for myself, was important to me. Whether she takes it down or not, I know the truth, and so does she. I'm really okay, Carter; I love you and am grateful you called."

"Love you too, Mom, bye."

Unbelievable, was all I could think. Revisionist history to clean up her past to allow her to launch a line of skin creams and whatever else Ted was up to. I silently reprimanded myself. This is what they did. Ted was a master at feeding my kids a cleaned-up version of what had happened to end our marriage. He blamed me for his behavior, saying that I had a tendency to overreact and was volatile. It wasn't true but his insidious comments had effectively driven a wedge between my children and me at times. They questioned how I would react to any bump in their lives and so had hidden things from me over the years. Despite my efforts to counter his narrative, he had successfully planted a seed of doubt in them about me. I wondered if that same narrative was playing out now. I went back to the kitchen, finished up my dishes, and then headed to the couch for another couple of chapters of the latest Tana French book I was reading, hoping to drive thoughts of my ex from my mind.

❖

Chapter 4 - Fire

As the October leaves turned amber, butterscotch, and deep hues of crimson, I embraced the Bell Harbor life I had adopted. Friday lunches at the Blue Dog Cafe became a regular gathering of new friends, which included Megan and Sarah, much to my delight. Jim Raven turned out to be the self-appointed group leader and planned countless events beyond just the regular lunches that kept me and the rest of the group busy most weekends. Together, we attended flea markets and farmers' markets in villages all around us and even went apple picking, which led to apple sauce, apple butter, and hand pies that I froze.

The flea markets had supplied a couple of end tables and nightstands that I still needed for my house and even some knick-knacks that I really didn't need at all. At the farmers markets in the area, I discovered a bunch of local vendors I had come to love. Two of my favorites were a small bakery that made wonderful sourdough doughnuts and a nearby farm that curated weekly baskets of vegetables. Although I wasn't always sure what the vegetables were or how to use them, they were pushing me out of my cooking comfort zone, and for that, I was grateful. Admittedly, the recipes weren't always my favorite, but I vowed to keep trying with each new basket of produce that I brought home.

On many of the outings, I noticed that Megan and Jim paired off. I secretly wondered if he wasn't planning all of the activities to continue to see Megan as often as possible. I had asked Megan about Jim once in conversation, and she brushed my innuendo away, saying they were just good friends, fanning her hand at my suggestion. I let it lie but continued to watch them together with growing happiness for her.

I felt at home on the small university campus and was enjoying rediscovering myself without my children. I kept my thrice-a-week jog but added yoga at the university gym whenever I could. I was also settling into teaching and developing a good rapport with my students as we explored the criminal mind together. I was using case studies to have them explore criminal behavior in the context of law enforcement over time. We had fun, and the students all stayed engaged.

On Nutmeg Hill, I had successfully tamed my garden, trimmed back the hydrangea border, and planted the beds lining the wrap-around porch with a mix of annuals, perennials, and evergreens to keep some structure and color during the winter. I painted the large living room a pale blue and the fireplace a crisp white, bringing out the coastal feel I had dreamed of when I first saw the space. I painted the kitchen cabinets white after watching a YouTube video and used the savings from doing the work myself to splurge on quartz countertops with the look of marble. I hired a local handyman whose card I found on the co-op corkboard to put up a subway tile backsplash in watery blue. I hung paint drop cloths, lined with grosgrain ribbon, as curtains in the living and bedrooms and let them puddle on the floor. Walking in the front door at the end of the day felt like coming home in a way it hadn't for years. I couldn't wait to show my kids when they visited for Thanksgiving.

I was deep in the Op-Ed section of the *Chronicle* when the phone rang on Sunday morning, "Ms. Glass?" a strong voice asked.

"This is she," I replied.

"This is Detective Finnegan of the Bell Harbor Police Department. I'm afraid there's been a fire at your storage locker. Can I ask you to come down to Stor-it-All and meet me?"

"Oh my God, was anyone hurt?"

"No. It happened very early this morning, and the damage was limited to just a few lockers. But I'd appreciate you coming down to the scene."

"Absolutely. I can leave in 15 minutes, be there in about 30?"

"That'd be great. Thank you, Ms. Glass."

***

I drove through town and out to Windham Road, where the Stor-It-All sat. It seemed lonely in this isolated part of town, as though it had settled there before it realized no other business would join it on this stretch of road. Although, I suppose that was where storage lockers were usually found. When I pulled up to the long, low building, black smoke was still rising in a plume from the end of the block. The right third of the structure had melted and twisted partially away and been coated in black soot. Everything dripped with water, and a putrid smell hung in the air. Two fire trucks were still at the scene, along with a handful of police cars. Uniformed men and women milled about in clusters while two others, in all-white hazmat suits, moved in and out of the wreckage. A silver-haired man walked toward my car wearing a brown herringbone sports coat and sky-blue tie, which

I noticed seemed to pick up the color of his bright, blue eyes as he leaned toward my window. His hair was cut short and had started to recede on either side of a strong front peak. It looked towel-dried and finger-combed and laid haphazardly on his head. He must have noticed my hesitation as I began to roll down my window because he reached into his pocket and flipped open his wallet to reveal his detective's shield.

He said, "Detective Mike Finnegan, I assume you are Margaret Glass?"

"Yes, and please call me Maggie. Is it okay to park here? I wasn't sure."

"Absolutely, please come with me, Maggie."

After I parked, we walked around the back of the building to the remnants of my storage space. I wasn't prepared for what I saw. It was mostly gone. My childhood desk, the dollhouse my father had built for me when I was ten and that I had repainted for my daughters and hoped to repaint again one day for theirs; baby clothes I had remade into quilts for my kids to wrap their babies in; school papers the kids had brought home to me that I had treasured; the kids' favorite children's books I had saved to send to them when the time was right; special Christmas decorations - all gone. An old exercise bike had melted over some boxes that had been next to it - maybe they could be saved. But even they were drenched in water. And the smell. The horrific smell of a fire that consumes your memories is impossible to describe. It doesn't smell like burning wood or plastic. It's the smell of loss. They say fire "consumes," and now I understand why. My knees buckled, and just before I hit the pavement, Detective Finnegan caught me.

"Whoa! I've got you, Maggie. Why don't we go back to my office to sit and talk away from all this?"

I nodded in agreement and thanked him.

He drove me to the police station. Once there, he handed me a mug of coffee with a little milk, just as I had requested. I slid back into the chair opposite him. Detective Finnegan sat behind a well-worn wooden desk with papers and files stacked in heaps that lined the perimeter. He smiled as he noticed my eyes traveling over the wall of clutter.

"Like my filing system? Trust me, I can find anything I need," he said, curling up one side of his mouth.

"I'm sure you can. No judgment," I smiled back. "I'm sorry I got so upset at the storage lockers, Detective Finnegan. All my kids' baby things were in there, as well as all of my childhood memorabilia that I was saving."

"Everyone calls me Finn; why don't you do that, too?"

"Okay then, Finn," I said and took another sip of the warm brew. "What happened?"

"Well, that's what I'm trying to figure out. That's why I wanted to talk to you."

"To me? Why me?"

"Well, it looks like the fire started in your locker."

"My locker? Was there a plug or light fixture that was faulty or something?"

"No. It was started on purpose; an accelerant was used."

"On purpose? In my locker? Why would anyone want to do that? To burn my children's things? My things?"

"Well, can you think of anyone who might want to do that?"

"No, that's crazy," I said, shaking my head. "You must be mistaken. Maybe someone got the wrong locker? This just has to be a mistake."

"Did you have anything valuable in the locker that could have been stolen?"

"Stolen? I thought you said it was a fire?"

"Your lock was cut prior to the fire, but we believe the perpetrator may have been interrupted by some teenagers who were drinking in the parking lot. We can see the kids on CCTV."

"Did you see the person who started the fire on the cameras too?"

"No, he or she avoided them."

"So, someone broke into my locker and then burned it? Did they take things from anyone else's locker?"

"That's the thing, Maggie, yours is the only lock that was cut."

"I don't understand. What could someone possibly want in my locker?"

"That's why we're talking - to figure that out together. Can you tell me what you stored in your space?"

"Memorabilia; my children's baby things and furniture I was too nostalgic about to give away; a dollhouse my father built for me; old photo albums - mainly stuff I knew I wanted to keep but that I didn't have room to store in my home. Lots of Christmas decorations, too. Oh God, all the ornaments are gone. I hadn't thought of that before," I paused to regain my composure, before continuing, "But certainly nothing of value to anyone but me and my children. That's why this has to be a mistake."

"Nothing else?"

"Not that I can think of."

"Okay. Well, the investigation is just getting started. Maybe you're right, and this is all a mistake. But I'd like you to write down an inventory of what was in that locker for me, please. I'm looking at all angles and don't want to dismiss anything."

"Of course. I'll do my best to try and remember everything."

"Thank you for your help, Maggie. I'll drive you back to your car."

"Thank you, Finn. Honestly, I'm a little embarrassed at my dramatic reaction today. I was a New York City prosecutor in a former life. It's just very different when your role changes, I guess."

"A prosecutor? Wow. What do you do now?"

"I teach Criminology at Eastern Connecticut. I guess I could use this as a case study for my class... once I get a little distance and perspective. Actually, I'd love to have you come to be a guest lecturer one day, not about this case, just about your work in general. Would you ever be willing to do that?"

"Sure, why not? I just have to clear it with my Chief."

"Thanks, Finn, that would be great."

Once back at the Stor-it-All, Finn dropped me at my car and said he would follow up the next day with the paperwork I needed to complete.

I drove home and spent the afternoon intermittently crying and angry at whoever did this, trying to pull myself together before calling my kids. Just before dinner time, I called a family meeting and poured a glass of wine to calm my nerves. Their faces popped up on FaceTime - Carter, Ruby, and Meryl - the loves of my life. A "family meeting" usually meant an important decision needed to be made so they were ready and attentive for what was to come, but their moods shifted when they saw my face.

"What happened? Are Nana and Gramps, okay?" asked Carter, taking charge immediately.

"They're both fine; everyone is fine," I answered. Then I swallowed and said, "There's been a fire at our storage locker."

Then my grief came tumbling out again as I saw my kids' faces before me and mourned again for all that had been lost that day.

"It'll be okay, Mom," said Meryl. "Do you want me to come home?"

"No, no, I'm just being dramatic. I know they are just things, and I am grateful that no one was hurt. But we lost all of your baby things, your favorite books, the special toys, your baby blankets, the quilts I had made for each of you out of your baby clothes, the doll house Gramps made for me, our Christmas decorations, everything. I'm just so sad."

"Maybe I could come next weekend," offered Ruby. "I'm just at Wesleyan, not as far away as Meryl at Emory or Carter in D.C."

"You're sweet, but I'm fine, and you'll all be here for Thanksgiving in a month. I just wanted you to know because they were your things, too. We have each other, and I know that's what's important - not material things. I love you all very much."

"I love you too," they all said in near unison.

We changed the subject, talked about the plans for Thanksgiving break, and debated at some length over which stuffing recipe would prevail. They each shared updates about friends and classes, and after nearly an hour, when we hung up, I felt almost like myself again. Pumpkin and I went out and sat on the porch swing, huddled together under a blanket. Watching the lights of the town sparkle against the river in the crisp autumn air, I felt as though I had been cut adrift. With my past now consumed, the only thing left for me was what lay ahead. And I thought of the song I had heard for the first time so many years before, *"Today is where your book begins; the rest is still unwritten."*

❖

Chapter 5 - The Fingerprint

Detective Finnegan knocked on my open office door as he leaned in saying, "Good afternoon, Professor Glass; how are you doing today?"

"Oh Finn, hi, I'm okay, thanks. And it's Maggie; please come in and sit," I said as I stood to welcome him into my small space.

Finn came in, closed the door behind him, and sat in the chair opposite my desk. He wore a mocha brown leather pea coat, like my granddaddy used to wear, over the same brown sport coat he had on the day before but with a grass green knit tie today, loosened at the neck. He held a file in his lap.

"I brought along the paperwork to complete for the burglary and arson," he said.

"Wow, it sounds really serious with those labels. I called my insurance this morning, and they said I needed a complaint number for them to begin my claim. Although, honestly, I'm not sure what can be replaced; it was all sentimental value."

"I wondered if I could ask you a few more questions for the paperwork?"

"Of course."

He opened his file and rested it on the edge of my desk. He pulled a pen from his inner jacket pocket and leaned over the form, asking "Full name?"

"Margaret Glass. I don't know if this is relevant, but I've just changed my name, so if you need to check it or anything, it could come up as

Melody."

"Oh, and why is that?"

"I was divorced. It was 15 years ago, but I waited until all my kids went off to college to take back my maiden name. I was taking this new job and moving to a new town, so it seemed like good timing."

"Understood. We won't need to check, but thanks for telling me in case it comes up in our investigation. The divorce was 15 years ago, you said?"

"Yes"

"Amicable?"

"No, not at all. But thankfully, ancient history."

"Got it. I understand ancient history. I was married for a year; it was a lifetime ago. We were both too young and knew it immediately. She is still a friend and lives out in California with her husband and kids."

"I can't say my ex and I are friends, but he is remarried and still living down in Ft. Lauderdale. I think our divorce was harder because the kids kept us tied to one another so we couldn't just walk away."

"So, new job, new home?"

"Yep. Trying something just for me. I've always loved this part of the country. I went to college in Maine and have romanticized New England coastal towns ever since. My parents are in New York City, and I want to be near them in case they ever need me, so Connecticut was a natural place to look for a job. When I found this opportunity here at Eastern Connecticut, it felt made to order."

"Sounds like quite a move you've made, in a lot of ways."

Finn cleared his throat and shuffled his paperwork, breaking eye contact with me, before continuing, "I got your address from Stor-It-All but want to confirm."

"349 Nutmeg Hill, Bell Harbor," I answered.

"When I saw the address, I wondered. So, you're the one who bought that old farmhouse? I've been watching it slowly come back to life. I live two blocks over on Windward Street. It's such a great old house. I love the roof line, all the gables, and the stained-glass windows in the cupola. Do they shine down inside the space? I've always wondered about that."

"They do," I smiled at his interest in the house. "It's been a labor of love so far. I was lucky it was run down because it meant I could afford it, as well as its wonderful view and garden. You're welcome to stop by sometime and take a closer look."

"Be careful what you offer; I really will take you up on it."

"The offer is sincere, detective. You've been so kind and patient with me with all of this mess; it's the least I can do."

"Maggie, I'm just doing my job, and it's Finn."

"Okay, Finn. Are you off duty this Saturday for lunch? If so, I have planned to try a New England clam chowder recipe. You know, when in Rome."

I shrugged and then continued, adding, "If you're willing to pitch in and chop a little, I could give you a tour of the house while the chowder simmers."

"Deal," he said, leaning across my desk and shaking my hand to seal it.

We finished up the paperwork, I shared the inventory list I had created, and Finn tapped his file against the desk to straighten its contents.

"One other thing, Maggie. I know you were worried about why your storage locker was targeted. It's always hard with fires; the blaze literally consumes the evidence, but we did find a partial fingerprint on the hard plastic frame of your exercise bike. Maybe the perp moved it out of the way when he searched your locker. Anyway, we don't think it's just a random print because it links to another arson dating back ten years. It's way too early to draw conclusions, but I know you were worried, so I wanted to put your mind to rest. We don't think this has anything to do with you anymore. We're checking who had the space before you and some other leads."

"Ten years? It's lucky you still had the fingerprint, isn't it?"

"Actually, it's linked to a case out of Texas, an arson-homicide. The only reason the fingerprint is still around is that one of those free defense clinics out of Yale Law School picked up the case and is helping the convict appeal his death sentence."

"I don't understand. Someone was convicted with that fingerprint?"

"No, the fingerprint doesn't match anyone in the original case or get a hit on the national database. Plus, we eliminated it as one of your prints, which were still on file from your time in the prosecutor's office. The clinic lawyers are all over it, and I've already had a call from the Dallas County prosecutor's office today. Could point to an accomplice."

"Or to his innocence? I assume that's what the clinic lawyers will argue?"

"I see the former prosecutor in you coming out," he smiled. "Either way, my paperwork will get a lot of scrutiny, so I appreciate your help. Our investigation is looking into links between the perp in the first case, this area, and his known associates. We'll figure it out."

"I have to say my mind has been spinning. I called my kids last night, and they were all offering to fly in. They'll be relieved that it has nothing to do with us. Thanks so much, Finn. Now lunch on Saturday can be even more relaxed, at least for me," I said with a smile. "Noon work?"

"I'm glad and look forward to it; by then, I'll need a break from all of this. See you on Saturday."

❖

Chapter 6 - Chowder

It was a beautiful Saturday morning as October drew to a close. Pumpkin supervised as I swept the leaves that had found refuge overnight in the spindles of the railing and the corners of the porch. Her namesake gourds were arranged on the steps leading to our front door, carved in happy, toothless faces. I arranged my coffee, Chronicle, iPad, and a bowl of warm oatmeal on the small table by the porch swing and settled in under a blanket as Pumpkin made her way up next to me. We watched as the sun rose in the sky over Bell Harbor, and the town awoke. I worked my way through the paper and responded to some emails from friends I had been saving up for longer and more chatty responses. I looked up the chowder recipe that I had planned and jotted down the ingredient list, plus what I would need for a side salad, some crusty bread, and a good bottle of dry white wine. I cleared up the porch, took my dishes to the kitchen, and got ready for my day.

I bundled up in a warm jacket, scarf, and hat, and then bicycled down to the co-op and picked up most of the ingredients I needed. I left my bike locked in front of the grocery and walked over to Grounded. Megan was behind the counter.

"Morning!" she sang out as I walked in.

"Morning!"

"Chai Soy Latte?"

"Not today, just stopping by to say hello. I'm making my first New England Clam Chowder for lunch and am picking up the ingredients," then, I dropped in as calmly as I could, "Detective Finnegan is coming over to see the house."

I smiled, and she came around the counter. There was only one other customer in the shop at the time and Natalie was helping her. But Bell Harbor was small, and Megan was a good friend, so she lowered her voice, "Detective Finnegan, as in the detective investigating your case?"

"Yes. He said he's always wanted to see inside the house."

"I'll just bet he has," said Megan with a wink. We both laughed, and I stayed another few minutes while we chatted until a carload of customers tumbled in, and Megan was needed behind the counter again.

I gathered my bike and peddled to the Fish Market by the docks for the fresh clams and fish stock I needed for the chowder. Then I cycled over to the liquor store for a bottle of white wine and finally to Sarah's boulangerie for a fresh loaf of bread. With my basket and backpack full, I peddled back up Nutmeg Hill.

I set the dining table for two and but decided it looked too much like a date. I changed out the placemats and napkins to look more like a picnic and took the candles off the table - even though they usually lived there. I replaced them with a beautiful blue ceramic bowl with all the colors of the New England sea and decided I was ready just as my doorbell chimed. I ran my fingers through my hair, trying to tame it behind my ears while pushing my bangs out of my eyes, and opened the door.

Finn had on jeans with the pea coat I had seen before and a collegiate striped scarf in shades of blue tied around his neck. His face was flushed, and he breathed clouds into the cold air.

"I walked," he said by way of explanation.

"Come in, you look cold. Let me take your coat and scarf," Pumpkin greeted Finn with vigorous tail wagging and sniffing. Approving, she wandered back to her bed.

"This was my father's jacket, and it doesn't have any lining. I probably wear it further into the season than I should, but I love it."

"I get it. My Grandaddy had this exact coat - it's great," I hung up his coat and scarf and noticed he was still standing inside the front door, staring up into the cupola.

"The windows are just what I hoped. Did you open this up? All the exposed beams up there at the top?"

"Yes. This area had a drop ceiling I removed, and you don't want to know how I got up there to clean the windows or the energy loss caused by the lack of insulation at that peak, but I love seeing those old beams."

"And the lantern?"

"I found it at a flea market in Coventry and had it re-wired. I needed to light the stained glass at night but still be able to see through to everything from the bottom."

"I love it," he smiled at me, and dimples I hadn't noticed before showed just slightly on his cheeks.

"In here, I repainted the fireplace and walls," I said as I led him forward into the deep living room.

"And you moved in when?"

"Late August. But it's just Pumpkin and me, so it's how I've been spending my time. Elbow grease and paint, mostly. The same is true in the dining room and bedrooms. The kitchen was the most work."

In the kitchen, I proudly showed him the repainted cabinets, tiled backsplash, and new countertops. I walked him through the other rooms of the house, reveling in his appreciation of my restoration of the hardwood, tile floors of the bathroom, and brass and glass doorknobs. We were in my office looking at the window hardware when I heard his stomach growl.

"Oh my gosh, I'm so sorry; I lost track of time and totally forgot about lunch! I'm so embarrassed," I backed away from the window and rushed through the hall into the kitchen with him and Pumpkin at my heels.

"Maggie, no worries, I love seeing the house."

"I have everything ready for us to get cooking. Oh! And I didn't even offer you a drink, and you've been here nearly an hour. I picked up some white wine, but I also have beer, I think, in the back of the fridge; which would you prefer?"

"Which are you having?"

"I was going to open the wine."

"Then why don't I help with that? Wine opener?"

"Last drawer on the right."

Finn opened the wine as I laid out all the ingredients we would need and pulled an apron over my Irish sweater. I knotted my hair up into a bun at the crest of my head and turned to hand Finn an apron. He was standing smiling at me.

"Glasses?" he asked.

"On the table in the dining room already."

Finn poured the wine and pulled the "some like it hot" apron over his green button-down shirt. I had set up two cutting boards with the recipe between us. I cleaned the clams and steamed them along with the garlic until they just opened, and the smell wove through the rest of the kitchen. Finn drained, shelled, and minced the clams like a pro, reserving all the broth. I cooked the bacon and set it aside, then used the fat to cook the onions, adding flour and then the clam broth and fish stock I had gotten that morning. Finn carefully dropped in the cubed potatoes, and we left the hearty blend to simmer.

I pulled the salad that I had put together earlier out of the fridge and handed it to Finn with some tongs to put on the table. I wrapped the wonderful crusty bread I found at Sarah's in a linen napkin, placed it in a basket with a knife, and added it to the table as well.

"Now we have 15 minutes while it simmers," I said. "Why don't we sit in the living room?" We pulled off our aprons, grabbed our glasses, and went in and sat on the couch.

"You've done a great job making this into your home, Maggie."

"Thanks. It really feels like home already, even though I have only been here a short time. I feel connected to this space, as well as Bell

Harbor and the friends I've made since I got here. A real home is so much more than just a house; it's the community around it, too. How long have you lived here?"

"Me? I've been here about twelve years now. I came after I retired from the NYPD."

"The NYPD? Twelve years ago? What borough? I used to be a D.A. in the Bronx."

"I was wondering when you told me you were a prosecutor in a former life if we had ever overlapped in our service. I was based in Manhattan. The 33 Precinct, Detective Squad."

The timer went off on the stove, and I went into the kitchen and stirred in the clams, bacon, and cream. I reset the timer for five minutes and returned to Finn.

"Sorry, you were saying you left the Detective Squad in the 33 to come up here?"

"Wasn't quite that straightforward, unfortunately. I was shot."

"Oh my God. What happened?"

"We were on a domestic follow-up. We thought everything was under control, and my partner took the wife into another room to speak with her. I saw the husband go for something, but I wasn't fast enough. The bullet hit the artery in my leg. My partner managed to cuff the perp and then get a tourniquet on my leg to slow the bleeding. He saved my life. During my recovery, I decided a lifestyle change was in order and began looking for new jobs where the pace would be a little slower. Bell Harbor needed a Head Detective."

'Sounds like we were lucky to get you."

'I don't know about that. But I sure am glad I found this town. The way you described it feeling like a home so quickly to you - I had the same experience, and it has only become more so to me over the years."

The timer went off again, and this time, we both got up. I ladled hearty portions of chowder into our bowls, ground pepper over the top, and sprinkled chopped parsley to finish. We sat in the dining room and ate, talking less than before while appreciating our work.

Finn broke our reverie in the food, saying, "Mind if I ask a personal question?"

"Not at all," I answered, looking up from my bowl.

"You mentioned, when we spoke in your office, that this move was a fresh start for you? Why was that?"

"Well, I had a very difficult divorce and an even more difficult ex-husband. Since the divorce, I've been focused full-time on raising my kids and working to support them. I realized as my youngest was getting ready to go off to college that I had sacrificed my dreams for a long time for theirs. Don't get me wrong, I was happy to do it for my kids. But I'm not getting any younger, and I wanted to see what was out there for me. Coming here is my chance at something more for myself. Maybe that sounds silly?" I shrugged breaking his eye contact and looking down at my bowl.

"Not at all," said Finn, reaching out to hold my hand. "It's exactly how I felt after I was shot. A kind of 'is this all there is' moment. I came here searching for something, too."

"Did you find it?" I asked, finding his eyes again.

"Mostly. I love my work here and my home. But I haven't found anyone to share it all with yet."

I blushed and looked down at my bowl again, pulling my hand out from under his to take another spoonful. I shifted the conversation to Bell Harbor, asking about his favorite spots, restaurants, and town traditions. Both of us had second portions and used the wonderful bread to wipe the bowls clean each time. The salad on the side offered an acidic balance to the meal, and I knew this would satisfy me for the day.

When we were finished eating, Finn helped me clear the table, and we washed the dishes together. As I wiped down the counters and toweled off my hands, Finn thanked me for lunch and the house tour.

"Anytime Finn. This was really fun. And the chowder was delicious, thanks for your help. I feel like an official New Englander now," said with a toothy smile.

Finn reached out, lifted my chin towards him, and brushed my cheek with the back of his hand.

"Remnants of lunch," he said with a smile.

"Thanks," I blushed, wiping my cheek again with the dish towel.

"Could I take you to dinner next weekend? To return the favor for lunch?"

"I'd love that. I haven't had the chance to explore many of the restaurants in town yet."

"Okay, I'll figure it out and give you a call. By the weekend, I'll need a break."

"Finn, is that because the investigation has you busy? Does that mean you've made progress on linking the cases?"

"We're still working on it. We're looking at an arsonist angle. The guy on death row in Texas burned down his business just outside Dallas. They think one of the employees was sleeping in the club, got trapped, and died. The theory is that maybe he used an arsonist who is at work up here now. So, we're running that down. The Yale defense clinic is all over this, too. With all the eyes on this, we'll crack it soon."

"What's the guy's name on death row?"

"Steve Croft. You gonna check out the case?"

"Call it professional curiosity."

"Okay, but that's it. This is dangerous. We have a death in Texas and an arsonist still on the loose."

"Yes, sir," I saluted. "And you still think this has nothing to do with me? I'm safe?"

"Yes, so far, we don't have anything that makes us think there was a reason to target you. You were new in town and had just rented the locker. Most of all, there was nothing in the locker that would have been valuable enough for someone else to go through all this trouble. Don't worry. We'll figure this out."

Finn retrieved his coat and scarf, shrugged them on, and then, with another thank you and a kiss on my cheek, was gone. I stood in the foyer and found myself smiling. I texted Megan to stop by after work with a winking emoji and got a quick thumbs-up reply from her. Then I remembered Steve Croft and went to my office to research the case until Megan rang the bell.

❖

Chapter 7 - The Brass Ass

I slept in late Sunday morning after being up to the wee hours laughing and catching up with Megan. I updated her on the fingerprint link to Texas and the slow progress the police were making on my case. Then, with her coaxing, I reluctantly admitted to myself that I had a crush on a boy for the first time since I met my husband some thirty years before. The whole thing was complicated because the subject of my crush was the detective on my case. But that didn't stop us from dreaming up possibilities. I also finally got her to admit that she had a little crush herself. She and Jim had been out on a couple of real dates and, in her words, "were taking it slowly," I was thrilled for her, and we reveled in our new romances.

When I finally got out of bed the next morning, the autumn sun was streaming in my windows. I padded into the kitchen with Pumpkin at my heels and powered up my Keurig. After letting her out, I fed Pumpkin, and as she devoured her food and lapped fresh water, the machine brewed my first cup of coffee. I opened my iPad, turning to the research on the Croft case I had unearthed the day before but hadn't yet read.

Steve Croft had been the owner of a strip club in the suburbs just outside of Dallas. The club had burnt down in 2011, and, tragically, one of the dancers got trapped and died in the blaze after hitting her head. Trace evidence of accelerants was found, and the death was ruled a homicide as a result of arson. Croft was immediately a suspect as the owner of the club. I couldn't find much information online about the investigation, but he was arrested within two weeks of the fire. He had been married with a daughter who was just two at the time. Newspaper coverage of the trial named insurance fraud as the motive. Croft proclaimed his innocence at trial but did not have an alibi other than his wife for the night in question, the early morning hours of Sunday, May 15th. He had testified in his defense and had no criminal record other than a bad parking habit, which had led to his car being towed and impounded multiple times. Nothing about the case seemed to link it to anyone or anything in Connecticut.

My stomach twisted into knots, wondering if the coincidence I feared was real. Amber, Ted's current wife, had stripped at a club just outside Dallas, but I never knew the name of the suburb, even after our divorce trial. But I did know the name of the club - The Brass Ass. Hard to forget. It had become a running joke for trial watchers, and even my own lawyer had found ways to mercilessly mock the name throughout the trial. All I had to do to alleviate my fears that it could be the same strip club, was to find out the name of the club that burned. I took a deep breath to calm myself and continued to read.

I poured over news articles until I found one on Croft's sentencing. He was given the death penalty for a Murder One charge with the exacerbating and underlying crime of Arson.

The article summarized the trial and concluded, "If only the club had been built as it was named, it might not have burned, and Tiffany Schmidt would not have died in a blaze at the Brass Ass."

I sat staring at the words, trying to process the information. I pushed back from the table and stood with my eyes still glued to the screen. I read it again, "If only the club had been built as it was named, it might not have burned, and Tiffany Schmidt would not have died in a blaze at the Brass Ass," No, it can't be, I thought.

The fire was in 2011. Amber had stopped stripping at that club, as far as I knew, when Ted had moved her into "the nest" and started supporting her full-time. From all I had learned, that was while we were still married, sometime in 2005, maybe 2004. Or, given her recent Instagram post, maybe even 2003. At most, eight years before the fire, at least six years before. Still, the coincidence made me feel sick. I sat back down hard.

My mind raced. Should I tell Finn? Do I have an obligation to tell him? Even if I did, what would I tell him? My ex-husband's wife used to work there years before the fire? If I did say something, then he would have to investigate Amber and Ted as the possible link between that Texas fire and homicide and the fire in my storage locker. All I could think of was my kids and how this would impact them. Their father would say I had implicated him in the arson of our storage locker needlessly, and he might not be wrong. He had told them for years that I overreact, and he would say this was another example. Would he be wrong? My children would blame me for pointing the finger at their father. They would hate me.

But what about Steve Croft? He was on death row. What if he really was innocent? My head spun until I pushed back from my kitchen table again, pulled on running gear, and tied my shoes as Pumpkin danced, realizing what we were doing. Pumpkin and I ran down Nutmeg Hill and through town, puffing clouds of crisp October air until we reached the town green that ran along the Connecticut River. With each strike of my feet, dread grasped at me. Had Ted and all the chaos he represented in my life followed me here?

We circled the green and ran back to Grounded. I took a deep breath, trying to exhale my anxiety, and pushed the door as the bell tinkled my entry. The warmth of the cafe mixed with the earthy smell of freshly brewed coffee and the aroma of rosemary wafting in from the kitchen. A couple of bicyclists were hemming and hawing over their coffee order and pastries to go, while Megan looked on with a smile as I caught her eye.

"Well, this is a nice surprise!" Megan said.

"Pumpkin and I were out for a run, and I thought I would stop by and grab you for a minute. Is that okay? We'll wait outside until you get a break."

"Sure, let me finish up this order," she said as she poured foam into a steaming to-go cup and secured a plastic lid.

I backed out the way I came in and sat at one of the cafe tables on the sidewalk. Pumpkin laid at my feet and enjoyed the break. I tried to regulate my breathing as I waited. Pumpkin sensed my unease and leaned her weight against my shin. I bent down, wrapping myself around her and nuzzling my face in her velvety neck. I breathed her in and all the comfort she could give as Megan pulled out the chair across from me.

"What's up? Romance news?" she asked with a wink.

It tumbled out of me, "I wish. You're going to think I'm crazy. I think I'm crazy. But I need to tell you something and get your opinion on what I should do. I am really worried about potentially overreacting and alienating my kids in the process."

Megan reached across the table and grabbed my hand, asking, "What's going on, Maggie?"

"I looked up the criminal case linked by the fingerprint to my case."

"Yeah?"

"It was an arson of a strip club just outside Dallas," I paused and then continued, lowering my voice, "the same strip club where my ex-husband's wife used to work."

"What? You're kidding! Are you sure?"

"Yeah, well, I mean, how many strip clubs can there be just outside of Dallas named The Brass Ass?"

Megan laughed, "Sorry, I know this isn't funny, but seriously? The Brass Ass?"

"I know, right? It's so stereotypically a bad strip club name that it sounds like a joke. I wish it was. Unfortunately, it was a highlight of my divorce trial because of the amount of money my ex spent there and the fact that it's where he met his current wife."

"But go back; you said that club burnt down and is linked to the fire that burnt your storage locker?"

"Yeah, Finn said the partial fingerprint they found in my locker links my fire to the arson at the Brass Ass. That fire killed a woman who got trapped in the building, and the owner, Steve Croft, was convicted of the arson and murder. He's on death row now in Texas and has been for ten years."

"Oh my God. But wait, if Steve Croft was convicted ten years ago, how can the fires be linked now?"

"Finn thinks maybe there's an arsonist-for-hire that's still at work."

"But why would anyone want to burn your storage locker?"

"Exactly. I have no idea. That's why I was googling the Croft case and stumbled upon the name of his club. But it's not as straightforward as the connection seems because Amber stopped working there years before the fire. And here's my question for you - should I tell Finn about my weird connection to that club?"

"Maggie, first breathe. Do you know for sure there is only one club with that name around Dallas?"

"No."

"Do you know for sure that's the club where your ex's wife worked?"

"No."

"And how many years before the fire did she quit the club?"

"I'm not positive, but probably at least six years, could be up to eight."

"Okay, seems like you don't have a lot of facts to go to the police and accuse your ex-husband of something pretty terrible. Even if he is pretty terrible," she said with a raised eyebrow.

"Wow, when you put it like that, I think I agree with you. Maybe I'm overreacting, just like my ex always accuses me of doing. I need to calm down and get my facts straight. This could end up being nothing. I would have run to the police, my kids would have hated me, and I would have sounded like a deranged ex-wife."

"You're not deranged. A little crazy maybe, but in a good way."

"Ha. Very funny. Okay, so I have more digging to do. I just want to be sure my ex-husband hasn't dragged me into something horrific."

We agreed I would continue to research the case, and Megan volunteered to help in any way she could. We hugged goodbye, and I thanked her for the calming talk I needed. Then Pumpkin and I jogged up Nutmeg Hill.

Throughout the afternoon, I googled various searches trying to figure out if The Brass Ass, where the arson occurred, was indeed the only one in that area, around 2002-2005, when I knew Amber was stripping. The other thing I realized was that the name could have been the same for two different clubs if one closed and then another opened. That meant that Amber could have worked at one club that closed shortly after she had worked there and had nothing to do with another one with the same name, which later burned down in 2011. All these possibilities only expanded my search and frustrated me.

After first being amazed at the volume of strip clubs to choose from around Dallas, I quickly realized that I couldn't tell if there was another club with the same name that had gone out of business by the time of the 2011 fire at Croft's club. I also was having trouble finding out if there were multiple clubs in the area with the same name - like a strip club franchise or something. Do those even exist?

I poured over chat rooms of people discussing opening new clubs and the hurdles of obtaining Sexually Oriented Business licenses in Texas, better known online as "SOBs," I wondered if the acronym was a purposeful legislative poke at those opening the clubs and smiled as I looked for an SOB for another Brass Ass somewhere around 2002-2005. Nothing was digitized or publicly searchable online, at least not that I could find. Hitting a dead end, I went into the kitchen and turned on the stove to heat some leftover clam chowder. While the chowder was warming, I fed Pumpkin, who began to inhale the food, as I lowered her bowl to the ground.

"Chew, old girl, you can't even taste it like that," Pumpkin was too busy swallowing and licking her chops to be bothered by my commentary.

She moved on to lap up some of the fresh water that I had poured for her and then she laid down in the center of the kitchen floor, perfectly positioned to be underfoot. I sat down cross-legged next to her and scratched behind her velvety, soft ears. I had rescued her from the Humane Society when she was three. She was the only yellow Lab who hadn't jumped up on me but had still nuzzled me with her tail wagging affectionately. She was already named Pumpkin, I supposed, because of the orange stripe that ran down the center of her otherwise straw-colored back. Since she had come home with me, she had been my sounding board, confidante, and co-pilot.

"What should we do, Pumpkin? How do we find out if there was another Brass Ass?"

She raised an eyebrow without raising her head as she listened, and I awkwardly boosted myself off the floor. I ladled out my chowder and started to grind pepper when the crank on the mill broke.

"Ugh, Pumpkin, I'll have to go old school and crush some peppercorns myself if I really want it. I don't want it that badly, I don't think," I carried the glass of water I had poured and my soup bowl into the living room, and as I was setting them down on the coffee table, I had a thought.

Maybe if I went "old school" in my search, I'd have more success. I googled counties in and around Dallas; there were eight. That meant eight county clerks potentially had "old school" paper copies of terminated SOB licenses or licenses valid today showing a club that had been renamed. If I wanted to get this answer, I could either get on a plane to Texas or hire someone in the Lone Star State to do the research for me.

The doorbell rang, jolting me back to reality. I rose and padded to the door, swinging it open to a witch, Harry Potter, and a mummy yelling, "Trick or Treat!" I complimented their costumes and passed my pumpkin-shaped basket full of miniature candy bars all around. I waved to their parents out on the sidewalk, yelling "Happy Halloween" as I shut the door with my hip. Thank God I remembered to get candy. They were the first of a steady stream of trick-or-treaters through the afternoon and into the evening, which depleted my candy, much to my relief. The alternative was that I would eat the chocolate and then be forced to add more time to my morning jogs, which I was reluctant to do.

As I locked up the house and turned off the lights, I thought back to Texas and wondered if I should go myself, or hire help, and what the cost would be. Between teaching and my kids coming home in three weeks for Thanksgiving, I needed to figure it out. I also needed to decide if I was going to tell anyone other than Megan what I was up to. I concluded that all I had at the moment was a terrible coincidence, and there was nothing to share with anyone, especially if it would hurt my children, until I had something more concrete. All this was still running through my head as I washed my face and then climbed into bed. A text popped up from Finn.

> *Happy Halloween! Thanks again for lunch yesterday. Looking forward to dinner…*

I smiled and responded,

> *Happy Halloween to you, too! Hope you got treats and no tricks! And me too…*

I was extra busy that week during my office hours as students were stressed trying to get projects done and juggle exam schedules before Thanksgiving break. In searching options for the Texas-based research that needed to be done, I quickly found that I didn't want to splurge on a private investigator to do all the work for me. Instead, I would hire someone part-time to keep it all more budget-friendly. I found MaryJo Barnes, a private investigator whose advertisement had pulled up in my first Google search. Her ad stressed honesty and discretion, along with 25 years of experience. Plus, I liked that she was a woman. I guess I thought maybe she could relate to the predicament in which I found myself. I called the listed number, and she answered with a very loud "howdy" before listening to my details and the services required.

After discussing her rates and methods, we agreed she would pull paperwork while leaving both follow-up and any interpretation of what she found to me. We also limited her services to one week. The caps on both time and scope would keep her fee reasonable but give me peace of mind that I had effectively investigated. We discussed whether I might need to travel to Texas but decided that it would all depend on what, if anything, she found. Plus, I would need to wait until Christmas break for any trip. That delay gave MJ, as she preferred to be called, time to pull the records and do some digging. Luckily, the university had a long holiday break beginning in mid-December, so if I needed to go to Texas, I could be back before my kids came home for Christmas. For the rest of the week, I focused on my students and pushed Texas out of my mind.

Chapter 8 - Finn

Finn arrived at 6:45 on Saturday night, as promised, to gather me and walk down to Water Street for dinner along the river. He had traded out his dad's pea coat for a navy, down-stuffed winter jacket, which reached his mid-thighs. The same blue striped scarf I had seen before was tied at his neck, and a navy wool winter cap was pulled down over his ears.

He smiled, standing on my porch as my door stood ajar, rubbing his gloved hands together, and said, "You look great. Grab a heavier jacket than you were planning. I can feel winter coming."

I wore one of my favorite outfits that always made me feel pretty and confident. It was a knit skirt with a matching tunic and long sweater, all in stretchy, heavy, oatmeal-colored fabric. I paired it with stockings, brown riding boots, stacks of delicate, thin gold bracelets, matching earrings, and a long gold chain with a tiny turtle on the end in the palest blue. I invited him in out of the cold while I bundled myself into a brown shearling coat, pink cashmere scarf, earmuffs, and brown leather gloves. I grabbed my purse and turned to see him smiling and walking towards me.

"I admire a woman who dresses for the weather. Too many are chronically underdressed and freezing all the time."

"Well, I went to college in Maine, Colby, and that experience sorts out that issue for life," I said with a nod.

"Gotta get moving, or we'll be late," he said while striding out the door.

I followed him, pulling the door shut, and he offered me his arm. Then, we walked down Nutmeg Hill towards dinner. We were going to Sea Salt, an Italian seafood restaurant. I confessed to Finn that I wasn't sure what Italian seafood meant and so hadn't tried this place yet.

He smiled, then said, "Then you are in for a real treat. It's Italian food you would find in seaside towns and cities in Italy. Dishes Vincent loves from all over, including Venice, Sardinia, and Sicily. It's fresh seafood with handmade pasta and seasonal vegetables. If you've been to Italy, his food is the closest I've come to the real thing. He says it's because he procures his ingredients primarily from Italy and then tops it off with locally caught seafood. His wife, Lydia, says it's because he makes it all with love. I think it's a combination of both, but you be the judge."

"My mouth is already watering. Yum, I can't wait. How often do you go?"

"I don't go out on my own that often, but I make a point of getting to Sea Salt. I think it's special."

"Well, thanks for introducing me to it. It sounds wonderful - even your description is making me hungry." I smiled and laced my arm through his.

We walked along in the crisp night air, and I realized I felt happy. I didn't want to over-analyze the feeling, but I loved that I felt it and looked over at Finn. His Irish skin was worn with age, creased around his clear, blue eyes, and smile lines framed his mouth like parentheses. I thought he looked kind, even though I had learned from my divorce that you can't judge a book by its cover. This time, I hoped the cover told the real story.

Lydia hugged Finn as we came in and unbundled ourselves. We hung our coats in a closet by the door and were led to a table overlooking the Connecticut River. Lights sparkled on the opposite shore, and the candle on the table danced in response. House chianti was brought along with bruschetta, topped with fresh tomatoes, onions, and basil. The chalkboard menu listed not only the entrées but also the day's catch and available fresh vegetables for your side. I ordered fettuccine with bay scallops done in a Venetian style. Finn tried Sardinian-style Atlantic cod over pappardelle. While we waited on our entrées, we sipped the wine, and Finn asked how I was settling into Bell Harbor.

"It sounds cliche, I know, but I really feel like I found my home. I told you I had a hard divorce and then raised my kids alone. I think I was just surviving for so long that I forgot what living felt like. It feels great, and Bell Harbor is a big part of that - the place, the people I've met, and the home I've created for Pumpkin and me. I've only been here a little over two months, but it feels more like home than Florida ever did to me."

"It had the same effect on me. I also came here looking for the next chapter in my life; it's a special place." We toasted to Bell Harbor and new beginnings as our meals were served.

My scallops were lightly rolled in bread crumbs, garlic, lemon, and parsley and were perfectly seared. The pasta was cooked *al dente*, and then sautéed garlic and lemon were added as the base for the seafood. A confetti of basil floated over the top. It tasted even better than it looked. I traded bites with Finn. His fish had been de-boned and simmered in a broth of celery, carrot, onion, and lemon. Afterward, it was laid over the bed of pappardelle and dressed with a sauce of sautéed garlic, pine nuts, parsley, and a splash of vinegar. We debated which dish was better but easily agreed both were terrific. We happily provided our amateur food reviews to Vincent when he stopped by the check on us.

After he left, I said to Finn, "You can tell the food is great because we're barely talking."

"That wasn't my intention in bringing you here," Finn replied. "I actually am hoping to learn more about you."

"Me too, of you, I mean. So where do we start?"

"How about where we came from? You know I was in the city as a detective. I lived in an East Village walk-up which was the size of a postage stamp from the time I joined the force right out of college until I moved here."

"You joined the NYPD right out of college? You were surer of yourself than I was at that age. I still didn't know what I wanted to do with my life then. I think I went to law school just to delay the decision."

"I always knew. My grandad was a cop in Brooklyn, where I grew up, and he was a huge influence on me. That is why I went to John Jay to study criminal justice. He died before I graduated, but he knew my plans."

"I'm sorry you lost him before you graduated. He must have been proud to have you follow in his footsteps."

"It was long ago, but thank you, and he was; he told me so."

"I feel the same connection to my maternal grandmother - I called her Nanny. She was an immigrant from Scotland when she was just 18. She and her twin were meant to come together, but the night before they were to sail, their father had a heart attack. Her twin, Jean, volunteered to stay and come later. Nanny arrived, found a job in a factory, and made a life for herself with only a 6th-grade education. Jean never came. Their family was desperately poor, and she could never raise the money for the ticket again."

"What a story. I can see why your grandmother inspired you. She must have been so proud of all you have accomplished."

"She was. When I graduated from law school and got a job in the DA's office, she was my first call. I shared the exciting news that I would be litigating cases in court, but she didn't really understand. So, I explained that I was going to be like Perry Mason from the old TV show, you know?"

"That old black and white show, sure. Great courtroom scenes."

"Exactly. When I mentioned Perry Mason, she got very excited and said she never thought a granddaughter of hers could be the secretary to someone like Perry Mason. I tried correcting her, saying that I was actually going to be Perry Mason. She didn't get it, but she was so excited that I eventually let the difference go and just said thank you." I laughed at the memory.

Finn laughed along with me at the end of my story and then said, "Just shows how far you came in two generations; she couldn't even fathom it."

"I had every advantage that she didn't. She was a wonderful, warm, funny woman. I adored her. She said we would go to Scotland together, but she had her stroke and died before we could. I still haven't gotten there, but I will someday."

"That's how I feel about Ireland. No surprise my cop family is Irish. My grandad came over from Dingle in county Kerry. The town sits on Dingle Bay and is famous for its music. Grandad could play the fiddle, and during holidays, he would play, tapping his foot, late into the night. He taught me the balance of hard work and play and inspired me to make a move here and live my life before I lost it."

"Then Bell Harbor is very grateful to him. Are you musical, too?"

"I can play the fiddle, but not like him, it sang in his hands. But I have fun with it. Actually, I'm part of an Irish band, and we play gigs when we can fit them into our lives."

"Seriously? That's amazing! When do I get to hear you play?" I asked with a wide smile.

Finn blushed, "I might have oversold us when I said band - we're a group of friends who get together to have fun and play music, and if we can get someone to pay for the Guinness while we do - it's a win."

"Sounds fabulous. Count me in next time you play. Okay?"

"Okay, okay," Finn laughed. "But keep your expectations low."

"Too late, and I can't wait," I took my last sip of wine and smiled a toothy smile at Finn as he shook his head, still blushing.

We both protested that we were too full for dessert when Lydia wheeled out a cart brimming with sugary treats. After Finn paid the bill, we re-bundled into our coats to brave the cold winter night. We walked home with our arms wound together, puffing clouds of November air. Finn walked me to my door and then turned to me, placed his gloved hands on my cheeks, and kissed me. It was soft and slow.

"Thanks for coming out with me tonight. I had a great time," he said as he continued to hold my face.

I smiled, saying, "I had a great time, too. Thanks for introducing me to Sea Salt. You're right; it really is special."

"I'm glad you liked it. Let's do this again. I know another great spot. Say, Wednesday?"

"Sounds perfect."

"I'll get a reservation and let you know."

He leaned in and gave me a last, light kiss before he retreated down my front steps and into the night.

❖

Chapter 9 – A Gift for Gab

MJ sent a quick update Tuesday afternoon, saying she was winding up her research and would have a full report for me later in the week. She had been good to her word and limited her time and scope, keeping my costs low. I was relieved because I still hadn't decided how to tell Finn what I was up to. With no update from MJ, I wouldn't know more that I needed to keep secret from him.

Finn picked me up Wednesday evening, and we drove inland to The Mills, an old mill that had been converted into a restaurant. A winding, wooden footbridge took us across a flowing river from the parking lot to the front door. We sat at the window looking out over the old water wheel and the rapids of the water below. The mill still held the implements of its work, now as art on the walls and sculpture tucked around the tables. The low ceilings had the original beams exposed, and the worn floors were sealed to preserve the patina. Hurricane lanterns on the tables provided most of the light, and as I looked around, I dubbed it my new favorite place.

"How did you find this spot? It's terrific," I asked.

"I love old buildings. This was a grist mill beginning in the early 1800s. Later in its life, it was a sawmill and eventually a brush factory. The owners saved it by turning it into a restaurant, and the food's not half bad," he said with a smile, gazing around the room as he did.

We ordered cups of Rhode Island clam chowder, which boasted half broth and half cream to make it less rich than standard New England chowder, and then surf and turf to share. I ate the surf and Finn the turf. We shared a half carafe of house red wine and Finn regaled me with tales from his days on the NYPD.

"We were trying to arrest this guy but didn't have enough to secure a warrant, so we needed him to step outside his house. We staked it out but after a day, we lost patience."

"So, what did you do?" I asked.

"I called a marked squad car to come, and the uniformed officer pretended to issue a ticket to our target's car parked on the street. The guy came running out yelling that he was parked legally," he finished with a belly laugh, and I couldn't help but echo him.

We laughed through the evening, sharing stories from our past until we noticed we were the last remaining occupied table. Reluctantly, we rose to leave and made our way back across the footbridge. Midway, we stopped to look at the rushing water and the slowly turning wheel of the mill.

"Thank you so much for tonight. I had such a good time. The stories of your life on the force are hysterical. I would love you to come speak to my class," I said with a smile. "About the challenges you and your partner faced and how the constitution plays out in real life. I think my students would love it as much as I have."

"I'd be happy to, my Chief gave me the green light. Thanks for coming tonight. I had fun, too."

We kissed long and deep, and I felt like I was floating until we separated. We drove home along the dark, winding roads in near silence, enjoying the quiet company of one another. When Finn pulled up to my home, we kissed again.

"Thanks for coming tonight, Maggie," he got out and circled around the car to open my door.

I exited as well, saying, "Thanks for dinner. Good night," then I kissed him softly again before going inside to a waiting Pumpkin.

***

Thursday went quickly until MJ's email arrived with attachments.

> Maggie,
>
> I completed the search for SOB licenses in the counties in and around Dallas back in 2002. There were two strip clubs that used the name "Brass Ass" during that time. The one that burned and another that closed in 2004. I've attached both licenses.
>
> Let me know if you want any further follow-up from me.
>
> Invoice attached.
>
> MJ.

I opened the two licenses, and there was nothing remarkable about either of them. I was hoping for something definitive one way or the other. Unfortunately, this didn't answer the question about exactly where Amber had worked. I could either ask MJ to probe deeper or go to Texas myself. I reviewed the invoice and saw she had been judicious with her time and left some of my budget unspent. Perhaps this would save me a trip, I thought with hope. I responded,

MJ,

Thank you so much for such thorough and prompt work. Given that there are two licenses, is there any way to narrow down at which club Amber actually worked? If so, could you estimate what your costs might be?

Many thanks,

Maggie

Almost immediately, my FaceTime started ringing.

A woman I assumed to be MJ appeared on my screen and nearly shouted in a deep Texas accent, "Hey, Maggie! I thought calling was easier than all that formal emailing back and forth."

MJ's personality radiated through the camera as she smiled. She had pixie-style silver hair that was spiked off her head on the top, lots of dark eyeliner rimming her brown eyes, which blinked behind oversized, round, black glasses, and enormous pieces of turquoise jewelry dangling from her ears, neck, and fingers. Under the weight of it all, I wondered how she could support it with her slight frame. Her bright teeth looked even more so against her dark tan skin, which was leathered with sun and age. I liked her immediately, even more so for the help she was providing.

"Absolutely, thanks so much for calling. It's great to put a face with the name. Thank you for all your help so far. I've read through the licenses and your note and am struggling with how to narrow this down further. I need to know which of these clubs she worked at so I can determine if it was actually the club that was burned and where that poor woman died."

"That's easy. Hit the streets and talk to folks. We need to find folks from Amber's hometown who know where she worked. The clubs are counties apart, and in Texas, that's real distance, so it shouldn't be too hard."

"Is that something you could do for me?" I asked tentatively.

"Sure, darlin'. Won't be more than a day's work, I'd say. My mama always said I was born with a gift for gab, and it's proved to be a valuable tool in my line of work over the years."

"Oh, that would be great, MJ. It wouldn't make much sense for me to fly down for what you can accomplish in a day."

"Mind my asking what this is all about? Although sometimes not knowing is better than knowing, if you get my drift," she said as she gave me an exaggerated wink. Then she leaned in towards the camera, clearly expecting an answer.

"It's complicated," I started. "I'm worried my ex-husband was involved in a crime up here in Connecticut. If so, it would be tied to that arson of the Brass Ass in Texas ten years ago. As much as I dislike him, if he was involved, it would devastate my kids. So, I'm hoping you find out that his current wife worked at the club that didn't burn and shut down in 2004. That would make his involvement in both crimes really unlikely."

"Wow, that is complicated. But I respect what you're doing for your kids. I never had any myself, never settled down. I'll take a run at it over the weekend when folks are off work and let you know how I get along.”

“Thank you so much. I’m really grateful,” I said.

“Sure thing, darlin’,” and with another wink, she disconnected.

I couldn’t get her out of my mind all weekend, even when Finn and I went for a walk along the Connecticut River as the first snow fell. The crisp air and pelts of icy snow shocked my cheeks red, disguising my guilt when Finn asked why I was so distracted. Instead of lying, I changed the subject, asking him if he skied. I had loved skiing the Maine mountains in college and hoped to get back to it now that I was in New England again. He laughed at the zig-zag of our conversation and offered to learn, having never skied while growing up in New York City. I pledged to plan a weekend for us once the nearby slopes were snowy. As we chatted and walked along the rocky shoreline, I hoped I’d hear from MJ soon. I needed to know where Amber had worked, and then I could decide what to do with the answer. Finn pulled me back from my thoughts as he suggested different case studies for use with my class. After some debate, we settled on a pattern burglary case he had worked on. It would highlight a modus operandi for the class, and Finn could also discuss standard police procedure.

***

My answer from MJ came Sunday afternoon as I was cleaning the kitchen. FaceTime rang, and MJ Barnes’ name flashed on my screen.

“Howdy Maggie, how’s your weekend?”

"Actually, I've been on pins and needles waiting for your call."

"I'll hop to it then. She worked at the one that burned."

"Are you sure? You're positive?"

"Sure as shootin'! I spoke to her daddy. Who, by the way, is no picnic. But that's a story for another day. Found him midday in a biker bar. I saddled up next to him and got an earful. She had a couple years of high school before she left home, only to live in a by-the-week motel down the road a bit from the Brass Ass itself. No doubt about it."

At first, I felt sorry for Amber when I heard about the circumstances of her life, but then I pivoted to the implications of what MJ had learned.

"And you're sure it's the one that burned?"

"Oh yeah, got him talking about that too. Apparently, he knew of the club owner, and the trial was a big deal. Said he thought the guy got too big for his britches. Didn't seem to lose any sleep over him going to jail or even being on death row. Her dad's not a very nice guy."

"Did he mention anything about Amber and the fire? Or about her time there?"

"No. He didn't seem to know that much about her after she left home. There's definitely a story there," she trailed off.

"So, what do I do with this now? I think I had convinced myself there would be no connection between what happened in Texas so long ago and what happened up here. I guess I have to share what we found with the police, with Finn, I mean Detective Finnegan."

"Finn, huh? Sounds cozy."

I smiled and answered, "He's the lead detective on the case."

"Complicated seems to be your thing, Red. My two cents? All you know is that she worked there years before the fire; not sure what that gets you. We don't have any link to the actual fire or death. But I'll write up my report and get it over to you tomorrow with my hours. If you need anything else, I'm your gal."

"Thanks so much, MJ, for sorting this out. I'll be in touch if anything else comes up. I have to figure out my next step."

"Yep, no problem, I'm not going anywhere."

I waved goodbye, and FaceTime disconnected. I was left with my thoughts. Oh God, that was all I could think. I called Megan, gave her the five-cent summary, and invited her over. Then I grabbed two glasses, a good bottle of white wine, and a bag of chips and headed to the living room. Just as I had the bottle open, Megan arrived. She poured for both of us, sat down at the other end of the sofa from me, and said, "Spill."

I caught her up on MJ and more details of what she had found and then asked, "Now what?"

"You've got two choices, I think. Tell Finn now or do the next step yourself and then tell Finn."

"The next step?"

"Go talk to Steve Croft and see what the link could be - isn't that what a detective would do in the movies? You have to go to the source. Only by talking to him about what was happening at his club back then will you be able to figure out if there really is any link to you. You need to ask him about Amber, don't you?"

"Ugh," I sipped my wine. "I guess you're right, but I would need to go to Texas and figure out how to get in to see him. Death row visitation isn't standard. I'll need to go through his lawyers, I think."

"Geez, death row, that's scary. Did you ever visit anywhere like that when you were a prosecutor?"

"No, not death row. When I was prosecuting, the District Attorney refused to request the death penalty. I was grateful because we didn't have to wrestle with the morality questions involved. But I still had the horrible experience of going to the Tombs, as they're called, and even to Sing Sing."

"Sing Sing, I've heard of, but what are The Tombs?" she asked. "Or do I even want to know?"

"It's where New York City suspects are taken once they're arrested. The more proper name for it is Central Booking. They're fingerprinted and booked into the system there and then held until they're moved to more permanent facilities. I used to have to go there to try and get confessions from whomever had been arrested when I was on felony or homicide duty. It looks like an old mausoleum; I think it was originally built in the early 1800s."

"Sounds super creepy and incredibly depressing."

"It is. More than anything, though, it always felt tragically sad to me. All of these newly arrested folks are being held in cells that you have to walk between to get to the interview rooms. That walk feels like a mile, even though I'm sure it was actually pretty short. The tragedy of it all around you feels suffocating. I always had to fight the urge to run."

"Sounds awful. I don't know how you did it."

"I was young. Fresh out of law school and excited to be making a difference. I used to tell my mom it felt like I was in a movie," I paused, remembering. "Seems like a lifetime ago."

Megan raised her glass, "To our younger selves."

I raised my glass to her and took a sip.

After another sip, I said, "I can't stop thinking about Croft. All this secrecy is killing me, and now we're talking about me going to Texas? How do I keep this from my kids? Their father is all lies. I promised them I would never lie to them."

"Maggie, you don't have a choice. It's not a lie and soon enough you'll know if there's anything linking the two cases. They will understand."

"I don't know. I'm not sure I would understand if I was in their shoes. And what about Finn? I'm dooming a chance for anything real with him when it starts like this."

"He'll see the position you were in. Trust in the relationship you have built with him."

"It's new. I'm not sure it will stand this. I really like him," I paused and then added, "I haven't felt this way since I met Ted."

"You don't have a choice at this point if you want to protect your kids and still sort this all out. So, let's figure out the next steps. Okay? The sooner we get a plan, the sooner this will be all over for you."

"Thanks for helping me get to the bottom of all this and for being such a good friend. I just feel like this is a lose-lose for me. Everything Ted touches in my life turns to crap," I frowned.

"Well, let's come up with a plan that keeps you out of it this time."

We toasted the sentiment and spent the rest of the evening talking through scenarios of how I could get in to see Croft. I heated the pre-made mushroom tortellini I had found at the co-op and drizzled olive oil and freshly grated pecorino over the top. Megan went to a group of mason jars growing herbs on my kitchen windowsill, cut some fresh basil, and chopped it to top the pasta.

We sat and dug into our dinner, changing the topic of conversation from death row to something more uplifting. I was resigned to what was to come, and we moved on to town news and how Grounded was doing with the slower foot traffic of the winter. I also quizzed Megan about her and Jim as we cleared the table and cleaned up the kitchen. She blushed, saying she didn't want to jinx anything, but smiled and said she was happy.

I hugged Megan goodbye as she left and padded back to bed with Pumpkin at my heels. The next morning, I woke as the sun cracked through the sky. I pulled on my running gear, leashed Pumpkin, and we ran. If not for Pumpkin, I might have just kept going, but we turned at our usual spot and headed home. I showered, dressed, and went to work.

My week was punctuated by Finn attending class as a guest lecturer to discuss a pattern burglary and standard police investigation techniques, as we had planned. He regaled my class with the details of the crime scenes and the collection of evidence that established the modus operandi of the perpetrator, or "M.O. of the perp," in his words. The method of entry, time of day, and items sought in each crime defined the burglar, as did the fact that, somehow, he had always known the residents were out of town. These commonalities had been linked to a number of burglaries, which had been investigated separately up to that point. Once the police had established the M.O., they focused on how the burglar could have known all the homeowners were away.

"Any ideas?" asked Finn of the class.

Hands shot up. Liam, a keen student who aspired to a legal career, went first. "If they lived in apartments in the city, it could have been the doormen talking or other workers in the buildings," he said.

"That would imply a conspiracy of a lot of people because the cases were across a rather large neighborhood," answered Finn. "Any other ideas?"

"Common neighborhood stores where their absence would be noticed?" asked Josie, a slight girl with platinum hair in braids.

"Good idea. Everybody has their local diner and dry cleaner, right? Close, but no. Any other ideas?" Finn paused and then, when no more hands rose, said, "The commonality was the postal carrier who had gotten the 'hold mail' orders as all the victims were on his delivery route. That realization solved the case, and the guy is still serving his sentence."

Applause from the class met Finn's smile. I joined them and even added a "whoop" to the great amusement of both my students and Finn.

"Let's thank Detective Finnegan for his time," a few more "whoops" emitted from the group, mimicking mine, in addition to the claps. I dismissed the class and turned to Finn, saying, "Well, you're gonna be a hard act to follow, detective."

"Nah," he said. "You got this. They're a cool group."

"Yeah, they are," I replied. "I'm lucky to have them for my first class as a teacher."

I walked Finn out to his car, thanking him again for his time with a brief kiss on the cheek in case any of my students were around. Then, I retreated to my office to make my office hours on time.

***

Over the weekend, I distracted myself by readying the house for the kids and Thanksgiving. Pumpkin could sense my excitement in anticipation of the kids' visit and supervised me closely with an extra bounce in her step. I pulled all my recipe cards and made lists of ingredients, treats, and drinks I needed to buy. I raked the yard to show off all the work I had done to bring it back. I cleaned the house until it smelled of lemons and lavender throughout and added flowers and some evergreen boughs to my shopping list to make the house feel more festive. Sunday, after the house and yard were ready, I drove to the grocery store two towns over in Coventry, to ensure the better selection I needed for the Thanksgiving feast. I reserved some fruits and vegetables for purchase later in the week at the co-op and fresh bread from Sarah's boulangerie.

On my way home, after a successful shop, I pulled up in front of Grounded by a fire hydrant. I put on my flashers and ran in to say 'hi' to Megan and confirm the time for Thanksgiving dinner just in case the short week got away from me. Once I got home, Pumpkin found her place in the center of the kitchen floor while I unpacked, prepped, and stowed all that I had purchased. I expanded the dining table and arranged the flowers. Then, I had fun decorating with the evergreen boughs along the mantle and above the thresholds of each room. The rooms took on the smell of the evergreen and the emerging holiday season. I had even bought a simple wreath of magnolia leaves, and I hung it on the front door. Turning to look at my living room, I saw the crisp white mantle of the hearth adorned with greens, and I smiled. Bell Harbor and this house were now my home, and decorating it for the holidays felt joyous.

❖

Chapter 10 - Thanksgiving

On Wednesday, Pumpkin and I picked up Meryl at the Hartford airport and then swung down to grab Ruby from Wesleyan. By the time we all got back to Bell Harbor, the afternoon was gone, and Carter was sitting on the porch steps, having arrived by Uber from the train station in New London. I was over the moon to have them all with me and welcome them into my new home. I gave them each a key, the grand tour of the house, and then spread the table for dinner with all of their favorites. As much as I was looking forward to more friends and family for Thanksgiving, the meal I cherished was this one, with just the four of us. We drew out dinner, catching up and laughing until the candles burned down, and we rose to clear, wash the dishes, and clean the kitchen. I settled the girls in the guest room and Carter on an air bed in my office, and then Pumpkin and I collapsed onto our bed, happy we were all together again.

I rose the next morning and tiptoed out to the kitchen after peeking into each other bedroom to make sure I hadn't dreamed the kids had come home. I sat at the kitchen table and laced my running shoes before leashing Pumpkin and taking our annual turkey trot to make room for the evening meal. When we came back, Ruby was sitting at the kitchen table with a steaming cup of coffee, scrolling through her phone, her long legs tucked up under her and a throw blanket wrapped around her shoulders.

"Morning, Mom," she said without looking up.

"Morning, sweetheart. How did you sleep?" I asked as Pumpkin ran to her water bowl. After lapping half, she dribbled her way across the floor and settled at Ruby's feet.

"Great. I love this house, Mom. It feels like you already."

I wiped Pumpkin's dribbles with a paper towel, sliding it across th floor with my foot, saying, "I'm so glad; I love this house too."

I sat across the table from her with my own cup of coffee and begar to review my "to-do" lists for the day. It was already time to get th turkey started. I set the oven to preheat and pulled the bird from th fridge. I cleaned it, stuffed it with a savory sausage and mushroor dressing I had prepared earlier in the week, and tied its legs togethe to hold it all in. I slipped the turkey into the oven and started the firs timer of the day.

"What can I do to help?" asked Ruby.

"Could you get ready and act as sous-chef today? We have lots o chopping ahead of us. I'm hopping in the shower now, but you coulc follow me."

"Sure thing, Mom. That gives me time for another cup of coffee," she said with a yawn and a stretch.

When I reemerged in the kitchen thirty minutes later, dressed for th day in a green tartan silk skirt, cream Irish sweater, and brown riding boots, all my kids sat at the kitchen table hunched over phones with steaming mugs before them.

"Shower's free!" I sang out, and Ruby jumped up to claim her spot.

Carter and Meryl negotiated timing with her, and I got down to cooking. Over the next couple of hours, all three showered, dressed, and joined me in preparing the dinner. Carter DJ'ed the day, playing an upbeat mix he had created of mainly country songs. We sang, danced, chopped, stirred, and sautéed until it was time to clean up again before the guests arrived.

My parents had taken the train up from the city and arrived earlier than the others, anxious to see all of us again. Megan, Jim, and Finn showed up just after three, carrying wine and a covered casserole to add to the feast. Ruby took everyone's coats, Carter was in charge of drinks, and Meryl brought out a meat and cheese platter she had put together. We sat and chatted with my parents, who grilled the kids about how they were in between the pleasantries of getting to know Finn, Jim, and Megan.

At five, I was ready to serve supper and invited everyone into the dining room. The table sparkled with candles and my best china, silver, and crystal. Meryl and Ruby had created a centerpiece of fall leaves that wove around the candlesticks and flowers and brought autumn color to the feast. The sideboard was laden with sweet potatoes with a maple-walnut crumble; the savory dressing I had scooped from the turkey and then baked further to crisp the top; rutabagas cut with a couple potatoes to bring down the tart; overcooked green beans to honor my southern mother; cornbread; cranberries both whole and jellied; Waldorf salad; Ambrosia salad; my famous carrot souffle; and a fourteen-pound turkey sliced and garnished. It was all beautiful, and when we prayed to start the meal, I added how sincerely thankful I was for my home, family, and friends.

Over supper, after being pressed to share by my mother, Finn regaled us with funny tales of his misadventures as a New York City police officer. Megan matched him with crazy coffee orders and customer complaints, which kept us all laughing throughout the meal. As my friends and family joked and talked, I couldn't help but mentally step back to be thankful again for this gathering. It had been a few months since I moved north and created this new home and life for myself. I realized I had just been surviving in Florida since the divorce so long ago. I had been going day to day trying to raise the kids and pay the bills. Now, I felt like I was living, not surviving. I hadn't realized until this moment how different that felt and how much I wanted to maintain this new feeling and life. My mind drifted to Croft and Ted, and I silently prayed it would all amount to nothing.

I was snapped back to the present when Megan started to clear the plates to ready the table for dessert. While some of us cleared and Meryl washed the dinner plates, others brought out cherry and pumpkin pies and the whipped cream Carter had made earlier in the afternoon. I brewed decaf coffee and served it with slices of the autumn pies, which finished our meal.

After Finn, Megan, and Jim left, I drove my parents back to the train station. I returned to find all three kids in the living room, having just finished cleaning up.

"Thank you so much for your help today; I couldn't have pulled this off without you," I said.

"Of course, Mom," said Ruby, with Carter and Meryl nodding in agreement.

"I'm pooped and am going to bed. It's been a long day. Will you send Pumpkin to me when you guys turn in?"

"Sure," answered Carter as he scrolled on his phone.

I kissed each of them on the forehead, patted Pumpkin, and went back to my room to tumble into bed. As I was falling asleep, I smiled, remembering my feeling of gratefulness. Thanksgiving has always been my favorite holiday. The simplicity of making and sharing a meal with those you love could not be beat as far as I was concerned. Although Christmas is wonderful, I always struggle with how commercialized it has all become. Thanksgiving, to me, still feels unspoiled. The holiday is all about passing down family recipes and who is around your table. If only more days were set aside for just being grateful, I have to think the world would be a better place.

The next couple of days were quiet. The kids explored Bell Harbor and quickly found Sarah's boulangerie, the co-op, and Grounded for their daily specialty coffees. Carter offered to help with some house maintenance and went to the hardware store for the materials and tools to strip the old bath grout and replace it with a fresh bead all the way around. We all agreed it looked like new when he was done. Since his dad left when he was seven, he had stepped in as my helper, and although I was always profoundly grateful, I also felt guilty that he had grown up too fast. I had done what I could to handle things on my own, but the realities of single parenting meant I had involved him more than I cared to admit. As a result, we formed a special bond that I cherished. Household projects like this reminded me of the nuances of our relationship. I silently prayed he'd understand why I was pursuing the investigation of the arsons, both here and in Texas, and then shook myself back to the present with my kids.

Following tradition, we were supposed to set up our Christmas tree, but all our ornaments burned in the fire. The kids were worried about decorations, but I surprised them by having already purchased as many exact replacements as I could online. Saturday morning, we drove to a Christmas shop north of Bridgeport to get the rest of what we needed, including a life-size, electric, singing Santa. I replaced it out of love for my kids and tradition. During the day, the life-like Santa's motion detector triggered ho-ho-hos and a myriad of carols. At night, it didn't quite strike the same merriment in me. Santa had all too often startled me nearly to death when I glimpsed him standing in my living room in the dark, and he began to speak in response to my movement. As we loaded Santa into the car, I silently promised myself to unplug him after the kids left.

On the way home, we added a new tradition and stopped by a tree farm to cut down our own tree. With it secured to the roof of our car, we drove home singing carols and getting into the Christmas spirit. By Saturday night, the house was festooned for the holidays, and we sat in the glow of the tree lights.

"Hey, Mom, not to ruin the mood, but is there any news of the fire? Have they caught the guy?" Carter asked.

"No, not yet. They got fingerprints, but they are linked to another old case in Texas, so that's complicated the investigation. Finn is on it, though, and he says there's nothing to be concerned about. They think it was the wrong place at the wrong time, and our locker must have been burned by accident."

"What was the old case in Texas?" Ruby asked.

"It was a very sad case - another fire, but a young woman died. They convicted a man, and he's on death row."

With that, Meryl piped up, "Death row? That's hardcore. How can that case be linked to ours if he's in jail?"

"That's exactly what Finn is trying to figure out. I think the current theory is arson-for-hire because the fingerprints aren't from the guy who was convicted. That's why they are looking at who rented the storage space before us and other renters in case they targeted the wrong locker."

"Wow, that's intense," chimed in Ruby.

"Yep, and to complicate everything further, the convict was already appealing his conviction through a Yale law clinic. Now, based on this fingerprint match, his appeal has picked up momentum."

"Is Finn close to figuring it all out?" asked Carter.

"I hope so, but I don't think they have many leads. The important thing is that they don't think it has anything to do with us."

"Who was convicted? Do you think he's really innocent and sitting on death row while an arsonist is out there running around?" asked Meryl.

"Didn't you hear Mom; they think it was arson-for-hire. That doesn't make him innocent. He might have paid someone to start the fire," corrected Carter.

"Yes, that's what they think, I guess. His name is Steve Croft; it was his business that burned."

With my response, the kids seemed satisfied, and the conversation shifted to the logistics of getting everyone to the airport, train station, and school tomorrow and back to their lives.

When I got in bed, I couldn't fall asleep, worrying that I hadn't been fully truthful about what I knew about the fire. With their father's endless lies, I had always promised my children I would never lie to them. So far, I had kept that promise, and tonight, I felt like I had broken our pact. I wasn't sure what I would have shared - that Amber worked at the business that burned years before the fire. Who cares? What does that mean? It could just be a random coincidence. I needed to talk to Steve Croft. I would fly to Dallas so I could also meet with MJ and drive to the Supermax prison and its infamous death row. Maybe then I could get some answers. If I could do it all in the next couple of weeks, I'd be able to resolve my suspicions before I saw the kids again for Christmas. But first, I needed Croft to agree to see me.

❖

Chapter 11 - Croft

Croft was in the Polunsky Supermax Unit sixty miles east of Huntsville, Texas. I learned through his lawyers that he would be transported to Huntsville only for execution. Given the fingerprint link between our two cases, the Yale lawyers had agreed to our meeting as a long shot. Their only stipulation was that I would share anything I learned of any potential connection upon my return. Without asking directly, I understood they did not plan to go to the prosecutors or police because of my visit unless something important came of it. I knew I needed to be more transparent with my friends and family. Still, I also knew I needed to take this last step before I disclosed my suspicions, especially to Finn, which could trigger an expanded investigation.

The town surrounding the Supermax had grown only to serve the prison and left you with the same feeling of wanting to escape as the cement fortress itself. There was the ubiquitous Main Street that every town had, but this one lacked the charm you saw in some of its neighbors that I had passed on my way. It was as if the melancholy of the Supermax pervaded the pores of the town, and even the shades of color were all tinged with grey. Texas was known nationwide for its more frequent application of the death penalty, and this town seemed burdened with that reality. The heat radiated off the empty sidewalks as I eased my rental car through town. I decided on the spot that I wouldn't dawdle after my visit. The Polunsky Unit rose barely above the horizon on the edge of town and was built of stacked cement blocks surrounded by razor wire. A single iron gate broke the windowless walls of the block that baked, even in the December sun.

Memories of the prisons I had visited as a prosecutor came flooding back. I remembered walking the corridors with men yelling as I went by and praying that nothing putrid would be thrown at me. I remembered the horrid smells and the feeling of despair of those locked away. I had gone with frequency to prisons as a prosecutor to take video statements and coax confessions. I had disliked the visits then, but this felt far worse. Death row brought a feeling of despair that wrapped around me and was almost suffocating. I gulped for air and wiped my hands, now sweaty, on my pants.

"Pull it together, Maggie," I whispered to myself.

I parked in a mostly empty lot and peeled my legs off the pleather seats of the car to step into the muggy Texas air. I checked and re-checked that I had what I needed in my tote and then steeled myself as I approached the fortress.

I walked through a procession of gates, checks, scans, and searches until I was finally ushered into a windowless room. A small table was bolted to the floor against the wall, and a plexiglass window looked into a similar set-up in an adjoining room. A chair and matching telephones were on each side of the bisected table. The guard turned and left me, shutting the door with a thud, and I heard the bolt slide back down into its place with a clang. I sat with my mind racing and reviewing the questions neatly ordered on a legal pad that I wanted to ask Croft. As a prosecutor, I was a confident interrogator. Now, I was a victim looking for answers, and my professional confidence had evaporated.

The door in the opposite room opened with a clang, and Steve Croft shuffled in, handcuffed at the ankles and wrists. His gray hair receded but was slicked back and still moist. His skin, now sallow, was damaged from once being tan but hung on his face, and dark circles cupped his eyes. His stomach pushed against his orange scrubs as he sat down, and the guard locked his wrist chains to the steel link on the table and then left the room, pulling the door behind him and bolting it shut with another loud clang. Croft pointed to the phone.

After we both picked up our extensions, he said, "You came a long way."

"Thank you for seeing me."

"Not like I have much to do otherwise," he licked his cracked lips.

His brown eyes darted over me, and I instantly felt foolish for my trip. What was I thinking? I cleared my throat and began.

"As I said to your lawyers, I'm Maggie Glass, and recently, my storage unit in Connecticut was burned. Fingerprints were found that match some recovered at your club, and I'm trying to figure out what links the two crimes. I know the police and your lawyers are investigating; I just thought if we spoke, it might help."

"I'm not sure what you want to know, lady. It was all a decade ago, and I've been rotting in a cell since then. You really think a fire in Connecticut is linked to the torch of my club and the death of Tiffany?"

"Maybe, that's what I'm trying to figure out. Could you tell me about your club and what was going on back then? Why might someone else have wanted to burn it?"

"Don't you think we've thought of that, Nancy Drew? There wasn't anything. It was just a cheap strip club with cheaper girls. I was barely getting by selling watered-down drinks and working the VIP room."

"How did the VIP room work?"

Croft laughed, "You've never been to a club, huh? These dupes pay up to go into a private room for extras. Supposed to be only lap dances or a little extra skin, but we let them pay for as much as the girls would do, and I got half, more usually. Stupid chicks."

"But some customers spend a lot, thousands. They could spend that much on sex in just one night?"

Croft belly laughed, saying, "Lady, you're too much. You really don't have a clue, do you? VIP means they get anything they want. Anything." He strung out the word 'anything' into three long syllables, adding an extra Texas twang for emphasis. Then continued, "and then they bill it through the club. That's the beauty of VIP service. No stripper's ass is worth thousands; use your imagination. And best of all? It's all billable on the corporate card. What a scam," Croft laughed again, with memories darting across his face.

"But you don't sound like you got rich off the scheme."

"No, but I got a cut. Like I said, I got half of what the girls scored and then a cut of everything else. I let them use my back room, kept it clean, and provided security."

"Who's 'them'?"

"The VIPs and whatever or whomever they wanted."

'Do you remember an Amber Knotten who used to work for you? Had to be 15 to 20 years ago? I think her stage name was Babette?"

"Yeah. Wow, long time ago. Skinny girl, good legs but no tits, not a great dancer either. Think she lived with some of the other girls in the motel down a ways from the club."

"Was she friends with Tiffany Schmidt, the girl who died in the fire?"

"Oh yeah, the two of them were thick as thieves. Pain in my ass, always covering for each other. Tiffany was a better dancer but was sick a lot, hooked on smack, I guess. She only showed up at the club to work and get her check and then would take off to do God knows what until she needed cash again. Amber was never that great a dancer, but she worked steady, and then she was gone. A VIP took her up north."

"So, Tiffany wasn't around a lot? She wouldn't have normally been at the club after hours?"

"Nah, like I said, she worked for the pay and never hung around. I always thought she was on smack. She had that tilt they get sometimes and had even started to get the puffy hands. If she hadn't died, I would have fired her before long. Nobody wanted to see her strip any more, and she was too out of it to do anything else for me," he snorted, curling his lip, and a shiver ran down my spine, imagining what 'anything else' might be.

I tried to redirect him, asking, "The fire was late at night. Any idea why she was there?"

"Nope. Lawyers asked me the same thing. Maybe she was trying to rob the place. Told you she was bad news."

"Okay. You mentioned that Amber went up north with a VIP. Do you remember his name?"

"Nah, some dupe she conned into getting her out. Like I said, I wasn' that close to what went on inside the VIP room."

"Who was?"

"A business associate of mine. You know, a silent partner," he said a he made air quotes. "He had a piece of the club and, in return, ran the VIP room."

"He owned part of the club?"

"Yeah. He gave me the seed money to get started, and I let him rur the VIP room to pay him back."

"What was his name?"

"Everyone called him Tom. And I didn't ask questions; he was jus the investor and ran the VIP side of the business. I got my cut and stayed out of his way - a partnership made in heaven."

"Do you know his last name?"

"Nah. It wasn't that kind of deal. He gave me the cash in a no questions-asked kind of arrangement, if you know what I mean."

"But didn't his name come up in your trial? I mean, if you had motive as the club owner, so did he, right?"

"Nah, I knew better than to drag him into it; I've got a family. Or at least I did ten years ago," he paused, looking away. Then he jerked back to the conversation, adding, "Plus, he's got no motive. He needed the VIP room up and running."

"Your lawyer didn't try?"

"My trial lawyer didn't know, and these preppy Yale guys still don't either. And it's not up to you to tell them. Got me?" His eyes narrowed as he glared at me. As he did, I could easily imagine the fear of working for this man. What must Tom be like, who Croft feared enough to keep his name quiet even as he faced death row?

"Got you," I said and shifted my questions, looking again at my legal pad to steady myself.

"Did you ever see Amber or her VIP again after she moved up north?"

"Not her, but the guy stuck around. Like I said, he loved the VIP room," the edge of Croft's mouth turned up in a sly smile. "Why are you so interested in them anyway?"

"Just names that came up. What about Tiffany? Anybody interested in her?"

"Nah. She was a nothin', born and died that way," Croft snorted and leaned back in his chair, wiping his nose with his sleeve.

Wow, I thought, not a lot of remorse in this guy. Even if he didn't start the fire that killed her, he sure doesn't care that she died. I looked down at my notepad to be sure I had covered all the topics I had hoped to with Croft.

In the pause, Croft commented, "I don't buy for a second that a sweet girl like you came to visit me to solve a storage locker fire. Are you gonna tell me what the hell is really going on?"

"Nothing to tell," at least not yet, I thought. "A lot of things I loved burned in that fire, and the police found a fingerprint that matched one at your crime scene. It's got to mean something, and maybe, if we can figure out the link, we'll both get justice."

"Justice. Ha!" he spat. "No such thing," he seemed to snarl at the idea.

"I know it seems that way, but maybe this fingerprint is the justice you've been waiting for."

An almost imperceptible look flashed across his face. Hope? Despair? The door behind Croft lurched open, and Croft rose to be unshackled from the table.

Before he hung up the phone, he leaned forward, pressing a hand to the glass, and asked, "Do you think any of this will help? I'm running out of time. I had a family ten years ago. I still have a daughter."

"I don't know. But somehow, our cases are linked, and if we can figure out how, it might help you. I'll tell your lawyers if I find anything, I promise. Thanks for talking to me."

He shuffled back through the door they had pulled him out of to meet with me. The door slammed closed, and I heard the locks disengage from the door to my own room. I backtracked out of the maze I had come through, hurrying as if someone would try to stop me. Once in my rental car, I sat in the sweltering Texas heat, letting it warm me up and stop the chills that began as I fled the grim prison. Then, I gripped the steering wheel and turned back towards civilization.

Driving back to Dallas, I realized Croft had made me uneasy. He wasn't a man I normally would have crossed paths with, but now our lives had become entangled, and I needed to figure out why. I called MJ and invited her for a late dinner, leaving me time for the three-hour drive. She suggested an On the Border chain restaurant near her office.

When I got there, the bar was two deep with divorcees. The smell of men's cologne assaulted me when I came through the front door and the women were each made up for a long night on the town. I recommitted to my single status and looked around for MJ. She was in a booth over by the window. Her pixie haircut and bright turquoise jewelry made her stand out, and she actively shooed away men as I approached. She let out a belly laugh when I commented on the scene and waved over our waitress to order drinks. Once we had our margaritas, I recounted my morning with Croft.

"Well, darlin', you don't let moss grow, do ya'?"

"I just feel I need to know one way or the other. This is all too close to home. Do you think you could help me look into what Croft said?"

"Sure, I can, but don't you think his lawyers and the cops are all over it?"

"Yeah, but they don't quite have all the facts. I still haven't told any of them the link to my ex and his wife. And none of them have his silent investor's name, Tom somebody. I wish he had known his last name. Plus, something else Croft said today struck a nerve. The VIP room. During my divorce, it came out that my ex spent $10,000 at the Brass Ass - in one night. I couldn't understand how you could spend that much on strippers. My lawyer even asked Ted about it in his deposition, and he talked about lap dances, but it never made sense until today. What if that amount was for drugs?"

"I hear you, but who cares, Maggie? It was ten years ago. Who would care at this point? And why would anyone think something in your storage locker implicated them? Plus, ten grand for drugs? Was your ex a serious user?"

"He smoked pot in college when I met him and bragged that he had done more, but I never saw it. He said he gave it up when he met me. But I don't know what to believe anymore. I guess he could have been, but honestly, I never saw any signs of drug use."

"I still don't get why a drug deal ten years ago in a grimy strip club would lead to an arson of your storage locker today. Talk to me about what's in there."

"Just memorabilia. My kid's baby stuff, my baby stuff."

"No paperwork? Tax records? Property records? What about all your divorce paperwork - copies of those depositions you just mentioned where Ted talked about the lap dances and talked about the Brass Ass?"

"I have copies of the tax records we filed, but we now know they were all falsified, so I'm not sure what that gets us. We only owned our home in Ft. Lauderdale, and Ted walked out and stopped paying the mortgage immediately, so I don't think there's anything there. What I have the most of is divorce paperwork, and there are a lot of financials involved. Those used to be in my storage locker in Florida, but when I moved to Connecticut, I put them up in my attic until I could scan them and toss them.

"Well, I think we should still look at the tax records.But it sounds like your divorce records are a trove of information. And honestly, a juicy read," MJ smiled and winked, taking a gulp of her drink.

"They certainly are that. I guess they are the only thing that hasn't really been explored well; after all, the IRS has poured over our joint tax filings. I know Ted had liens placed on him by the IRS for hundreds of thousands of dollars. Other creditors also went after him. There probably isn't a lot left to find there."

"Okay, so we need to review your divorce paperwork. What could be in those records that someone wants to destroy?"

"Nothing, at least nothing that I can remember. Although to be honest, I was still so traumatized at the time of the divorce trial I don't remember everything perfectly."

"Then it sounds like it's time to read it. And if you're willing to scan it as you go, I can read it too if it would help."

"That would be safer, too - once it's digitized, it's out of my house."

"Let's do this. You go back and read and scan. I will nose around and try to learn more about what Croft meant by 'anything goes in the VIP room' and try to figure out who that Tom guy is. I'll keep my time to one day, two at most. If you find something you think is worth me reading too, let me know."

"We have a plan. My kids are coming home this week for Christmas, so let's regroup as soon as they leave for their dad's, just before the new year."

"Cheers to that," she said, raising her glass to meet mine.

We ordered veggie fajitas to split, with the best fresh guacamole on the side I have ever had. MJ regaled me with stories of some of her more interesting cases until I started to yawn. We paid our tab and then walked out to my car. MJ said good night with a bear hug and then turned back to the restaurant.

"Forget something?" I asked.

"Yeah, I think his name was Roger," she smiled, winked, and disappeared back into the bar.

I rose at dawn to catch my flight home. By the time I swung by Megan's to pick up Pumpkin, it was dark, and I collapsed into my bed when I got home. I was relieved the trip was over and hopeful it would bring the answers I needed.

❖

Chapter 12 - Christmas

Christmas night, I sat curled on the couch before the fire with only the glow of the tree lights. I loved the warmth of the fireplace and smiled at the earlier debate between Ruby and Carter about the perfect way to start the fire. Neither had been in the scouts, but both seemed to think they were experts. Meryl had sat back with amusement as her siblings had both gotten sooty, bringing in wood and stacking the logs. With the memory still playing in my head, I sipped hot cocoa as carols from an iTunes holiday station played from my new speaker. Carter came out from the kitchen, cradling his cocoa to join me and bearing treats for the top of our mugs.

"One of my favorite traditions," he said as he settled beside me.

"Marshmallows? Candy cane?" he offered.

"Thank you," I said, plucking a candy cane and slipping it into my cocoa.

We sat quietly as we sipped and listened, only periodically singing along to a refrain. The girls had retreated to their room to try on their new clothes and text with their friends.

"I'll be so sorry to see you all go," I said. "But you'll be back for spring break - or at least half of it."

"I don't know how that'll work, Mom. Dad says he's moving again. But this time, not just across town."

"Oh yeah, where to this time? He flips rentals like I change shoes."

"He says he's got a deal that if it goes through, he can retire. They're looking at property in the Maldives. But you know how he is, all talk. It might not even happen."

"Wow. That's the skin cream deal you told me about?"

"No, it's something different. The skin cream deal was Amber. This is Dad. He says it's his retirement plan."

"And they would move to the Maldives? So far away?"

"That's what he told me, but you know, Dad-" he broke off, sipping his cocoa.

"Do the girls know?"

"Yeah."

"None of you mentioned it."

"I think we all just don't want to upset you. Plus, Dad has lots of hare-brained schemes, and who knows if this one is even real."

"You're right—nothing to worry about now. It probably won't even happen. This time last year, you said they were moving to Savannah, Georgia. By Spring, you said Miami, Florida. I think Ruby even said St. Maarten at one point." I swigged down the rest of my cocoa and got up.

"Music on or off? I'm going to go to bed."

"I hope I didn't upset you, Mom."

"No, Carter, I'm just tired. Long day for Mrs. Claus," I said with a wink.

"Okay then, music on, please. I'll turn it off with the tree lights when the fire's dead, and I go to bed. Love you, Mom, Merry Christmas."

"Love you too, sweetheart. Merry Christmas."

Passing the girls' room, I knocked and ducked in, kissing them both and wishing them a merry Christmas. They were still modeling their new outfits for each other and catwalking in front of the bed. I was so grateful they were all home with me.

As I brushed my teeth, I calculated that I needed at least three more years of stability out of Ted for him to pay child support, which I used to help pay off some of the kids' college loans. Before I got too worried that he was running off to the Maldives, I reminded myself of all his other aborted plans I had been told about over the years and exhaled, climbing into bed.

The next three days flew by with the kids home. We watched *It's a Wonderful Life*, went ice skating on a pond over in Coventry, frequented Sarah's bakery, and stopped at Grounded almost daily for Megan's grind of the day. Most importantly, we completed our annual Christmas puzzle. We were late finishing it this year, as we usually completed it by Christmas Eve to have it ready for Santa to inspect. Even grown, the kids knew it was a prerequisite for gifts. I was lucky to have found a replacement on eBay after losing the original puzzle in the locker fire. It had arrived too late to finish before Christmas, but we all agreed that Santa would understand.

The four of us cooked big dinners that we lingered over, catching up on the minutia of each other's lives. We ended our holiday together by inviting Finn, Megan, and Jim to join us for a seafood extravaganza that we had created. We started with cooked, chilled shrimp and raw oysters by the fire and a fun, apple cider sangria that Ruby had concocted. Dinner was Maine lobster, homemade creamed spinach a la Carter, and green goddess rice I had made since the kids were little. The result was a green and red plate of food in full Christmas spirit. We opened our Christmas crackers with a bang, donned the colorful paper crowns, and read aloud our fortunes and jokes while booing or laughing, as each deserved. Dessert was a Yule log I had found at Sarah's boulangerie, and Rice Krispy treat stacks tied in licorice strings to look like stacked packages, care of Meryl. We hardly noticed the time until Megan exclaimed that it was past midnight and that she had to open the store in six hours. Finn stayed to clear the table and wash dishes with us, but we all insisted that Jim walk Megan home. By the time I fell into bed, it was past one; I barely reflected on how happy I was before falling asleep.

The next afternoon, Pumpkin and I drove the kids to New Haven to catch the Metro North train to New York. They could catch a bus from Grand Central to LaGuardia airport to go and visit their dad. I hugged them goodbye through tears and held on past when I should with the kids, each embarrassed by their mom's display in public. On the drive back home, Pumpkin curled up in the co-pilot seat and snoozed while I contemplated pulling my divorce files down from the attic.

I was dreading reading through the paperwork. I had tried it only once before, when my family encouraged me to get an annulment. The Catholic Church required such specificity in the documentation that I had poured over the paperwork of our marriage, including the divorce. It was so painful that I had given up. I realized now that I was procrastinating pulling down the boxes for fear of what I would learn that I had either forgotten or blocked out. But I knew I had no choice. So, when I turned into the driveway, I patted Pumpkin, took a deep breath, and resolved to read and scan the all the sordid details. I also needed to follow up with MJ to see if she had learned any more about those VIP rooms and who the Brass Ass mystery investor, "Tom," was.

❖

Chapter 13 - The Paperwork

Once again, the full-frontal assault of what Ted had done slammed into me. MJ had talked to former strippers to figure out what went on in those fancy, private VIP rooms. The depravity and seediness were more than my imagination had previously conjured. I remember after I found out about Ted's secret life and his affairs, that I saw my doctor for anxiety and depression. I was shocked at the time when he suggested a battery of sexually transmitted disease tests. Hearing about the activities of VIP rooms from MJ made me grateful for his advice. MJ continued regaling me via FaceTime with what she had learned and also provided the cost of everything she had described. She added a caveat that this was from the women's perspective that worked the rooms, so it might not be the price the clubs charged. This made the numbers even more staggering. Croft hadn't been exaggerating when discussing the money flowing in the VIP rooms.

"For a price, a VIP could name his sin, and the club owners would match him to his vice. Drugs, sex of all perversions, and crime moved through those dark back rooms. Depending on the ask, the transactions were either in cash or charged on corporate credit cards. All of the women talked about the money and how it flowed. That's what drove the VIP rooms."

As MJ spoke, I remembered Liz, Ted's former officer manager, telling me to "follow the money." I relayed to MJ a summary of the information that Liz had given to me, as well as what she had said about the money.

"There's your motive," said MJ. "Maybe Tiffany was blackmailing

Croft. Maybe she wanted a bigger cut to support her heroin addiction."

"We don't know that," I cautioned. "You're assuming she was the target of the arson versus just a horrible mistake - wrong place, wrong time. And what does old blackmail have to do with the arson of my storage locker ten years later?"

"But now we know the type of activity happening back then. Maybe that helps?" she asked.

"I don't know. I've got to read all the paperwork from my divorce. There's got to be a link between the crimes in there somewhere. There are depositions, transcripts from the trial, accounting, and everything else. I keep putting it off because it is so disgusting to read about my ex-husband and how he treated me and our marriage, but I've got to start, or I'll never finish. I'll keep you posted. Thanks, MJ."

"Sure thing, Maggie," she said and disconnected.

After tucking away my iPad, I entered the bedroom hall and pulled down the attic ladder. I precariously hauled eight jammed boxes down, balancing them on my shoulder with one arm while holding on to the ladder with the other. Once finished and sweaty, I set up my scanner and lined the boxes against my office wall. I filled a bottle of water and sat down to read. The boxes were daunting. I had tried to organize everything at the time, but the three-inch-thick, white binders were only labeled A-C, C-E… etc. There were several others labeled "Transcripts & Depositions," and one menacingly said "IRS" - it was four inches thick and bursting at the seams. I grabbed the one on top, "C-E," and opened it on the desk. It was an assortment of paperwork with no apparent link to "C-E." There's a deep insight into my state of mind at the time, I thought.

It started with documentation from Ted's company retirement loan program. As the company's owner, Ted had changed the plan's terms just after we separated, draining our retirement assets with his single signature. I remember calling the financial services company and complaining, only for them to tell me to talk to my husband's employer. I also remember hanging up on them.

Next in the binder was a *New York Times* article on divorcees selling items on eBay, followed by the receipts of all of Ted's items I had sold to pay bills until I could find work - totaling $5,738.12. It had been my brief and very cathartic obsession. My lawyer told me I could sell anything Ted had abandoned when he left our home. Ted had walked out with only his clothes - leaving everything else behind. So, I sold his watch, bicycle, golf clubs, book collection, bedroom furniture, and everything else that reminded me of him. It was a distraction at the time and raised much-needed cash when he emptied the bank and retirement accounts, cut off my credit cards, and stopped paying the mortgage. I lingered over my sales receipts and then pressed on to the even more depressing sections.

Next were my handwritten lists of account numbers - at the time, they must have made sense, but now my notations were like code, and the hand-drawn lines connecting the accounts were hard to follow. The next section had information from my divorce lawyer's private investigator, including Texas and Florida speeding tickets, threatened license suspensions, and court notices to Ted. The dates were all 2004 and 2005, which tracked with what I thought, and supported Amber probably being gone from the Brass Ass long before the fire.

I took a break and went to the kitchen to make myself lunch. I added a whole wheat wrap to a pan, some sliced turkey, and crumbled feta cheese on top, and then heated until it all melted together. I topped it with chopped tomatoes, lettuce, and some onion slices and sat at the kitchen table to eat. The sun was still streaming through the east-facing windows of the kitchen as Pumpkin ambled in, just in time to sit at my feet in case something dropped. As I chewed, I mulled over what I had read so far. How did I know so little about my husband? I always went down this rabbit hole when I thought about Ted. As often as I remind myself that he lied and lied well, I still felt I should have known. I shook myself from my thoughts, walked across the kitchen, brushed the last quarter of my wrap into Pumpkin's bowl, and dropped my plate into the dishwasher. After my break, I reluctantly returned to the office to keep reading.

Next were entries from the forensic accountant. In addition to accounting work, he had read through all the depositions. He created a table of contents for "statements regarding unsupported income in general," "statements regarding strip clubs as business deductions," and "statements regarding lack of spousal awareness of malfeasance." I suppose the last category was to build my defense for the IRS. At the bottom of the page were two asterisks.

> *Admits his 2004 tax return is fraudulent

> **Admits spouse was removed from joint American Express account in May 2006

I had forgotten about the second point and why it was necessary. I flipped back to the first section of the binder, and a plastic envelope held notes in my handwriting. When I had scanned them earlier, they hadn't meant much, but now I opened the envelope again, and the notes fell onto the desk.

Amber Knotten added to the account - $54,691.91

AMEX special research group

Credit report

Need to be removed

CANCELLED

Ted and Amber had run up our joint credit card, leaving me in enormous credit card debt. I had struggled to prove it wasn't me and to get myself removed. How did I forget this? I restored the paper slips in the envelope, sealed the Velcro flap to put it behind me again, and turned my attention to the first asterisk.

*Admits his 2004 tax return is fraudulent

I slid my pointer finger down the table of contents, looking for the corresponding page - 144, lines 2-21. I read the lines, finding them confusing. However, they must have proved the accountant's point because, in the end, the IRS had granted me Innocent Spouse Protection from Ted's crimes. I read on to try and get context for the accountant's conclusion, and several pages later, my lawyer asked where the money came from that started Ted's consulting firm. I had never asked how they had gotten the money to start the business. I had always assumed Ted and his business partner, Dwayne, had gotten a bank loan. I also had no memory of hearing these questions during Ted's deposition. The back and forth between Ted and my lawyer was jarring as I read along,

"Answer: When we started the company, we got a private investor, and he started- or we used that as a line, initial line of credit.

Question: That was who?

A: I don't remember his name.

Q: How much?

A: A hundred thousand dollars.

Q: And you don't know his name?

A: Well, it was through Tom Burke, so through Tom, I think it was his cousin. I'm not exactly sure. I'm pretty sure it was his cousin.

Q: Was money borrowed during the marriage?

A: Yes. We had to pay that back.

Q: And repaid during the marriage?

A: That is correct."

One hundred thousand dollars from a stranger whose name he doesn't know? I scanned through the following pages, and there was no follow-up question by my lawyer. Ugh. I would say I got what I paid for, but my divorce lawyer was expensive. I re-read the section.

I vaguely remembered the name Tom Burke. I remember Ted talking a lot about him when they were first starting the firm, but never about a loan, and then I didn't hear much about him anymore. I had assumed their careers had taken different paths. I know now that I had assumed a lot about Ted and our life, which was wrong. How did I not remember this, and why had I not realized what he was saying then?

More importantly, now the name Tom had a new meaning for me. Someone named Tom ran the VIP room at the Brass Ass and was also an investor there. Could it be the same, Tom? The coincidence seemed too much to believe. If he was the same man, why would a strip club investor want to invest in a small healthcare consulting business? Could it be as simple as a friendship forged in the VIP room? I knew I was missing something, but I didn't know what.

I went back to the divorce paperwork. I had been reading for an hour and felt sick at the level of dishonesty and seediness my ex was comfortable around. This was why I avoided these boxes like the plague for the last fifteen years. I had to try to distance myself and read like an investigator. I got up, rolled my head around, pressed my shoulders down, sat back down, marked the page, and flipped to the next section.

Amber's deposition was next. I skimmed it as the intimate details were still too painful to linger over. She said they met on February 14, 2005, at the Brass Ass.

> "Q: And were you a guest or an employee there?
>
> A: I was an employee.
>
> Q: A dancer?
>
> A: I was an entertainer, yes."

Yuck. This is why I never read this. But later on, my lawyer asked her,

> "Q: When you started seeing Mr. Melody in February, March, and now we're into April of '05, where were you living?
>
> A: At the Budget Suites.
>
> Q: In Dallas?
>
> A: In Dallas.
>
> Q: Was that one of those motels you pay by the week or something?
>
> A: Yes. Furnished. It's a temporary situation—week to week.
>
> Q: Is that motel just across the street from the strip club?
>
> A: Yeah, from the gentleman's club."

It was a pathetic story. If her sad tale hadn't blown up my life, I would feel sorry for her. Wait. 2005? Her latest Instagram post had pegged their relationship as starting in 2003. I added the discrepancy to my notes and scoured through the boxes until finally pulling out the forensic accounting binder. It had the details behind the accountant's summary I had seen earlier. Account numbers and columns of money movements filled Excel spreadsheets. One thing was clear to me: the money was not being transferred to our family's bank account. Over the years, our income dropped, with ever-growing amounts being re-routed into accounts to which I had no access or knowledge. Some accounts had Amber's name, but others were in Ted's alone. Some flows showed account numbers to which money moved and then moved again. That second move meant the accountants had no further information. There were also considerable withdrawals in cash from a number of the accounts.

I thought back to that time in our marriage. I had wanted to go back to school for architecture and was asked by Ted to put off my classes because we didn't have the funds. I had agreed and felt guilty for even asking to go back to school. Seeing the money movements now and knowing that the money meant for my tuition had, in fact, paid for Amber's aesthetician school made my blood boil. What a scoundrel. I shook it off and stretched back in my chair, scanning the notes I had taken on the accounts. Where did all the money come from? He didn't make that much – at least, that's what I thought.

I chuckled, chastising myself out loud, "Grow up, Maggie, you don't know anything about this guy. You never did."

Plus, the accountant had only gone back to January 2005 because that's when they said their relationship started, so there was no way to check the older money flows. Ugh. Pumpkin raised her head from her sunny patch on the floor to acknowledge my comment and then, realizing there wasn't more to come, settled back down to her nap. I knelt beside her, burying my face in her neck and stroking her velvety ears.

"You don't lie, do you, girl?" I breathed in her fur and kissed her head.

I went to the kitchen, made myself a cup of lemon verbena tea in my favorite mug labeled "Might be Vodka," and returned to my office. I ran my finger down the numbers again and pulled out my calculator. The total was in the millions. He couldn't have earned that much in a tiny consulting firm for hospitals. I suddenly wished I had taken more business classes in school to better understand the numbers. The staggering thing was the number of accounts and the continuous movement of the money. And then it hit me…. money laundering. But if his consulting business wasn't the source of the funds, what did all this mean? What if this was just my imagination? Was I trying to find something nefarious and seeing things that weren't there? I also wanted MJ to review the numbers and see what she thought. I scanned the accounting paperwork and emailed it to MJ, asking her to spend one day on it and then give me an opinion. I didn't tell her what hypothesis I had drawn. MJ texted about 30 minutes later,

> *Got it and on it.*

It was also crystal clear to me that it was time to tell Finn. I texted,

> *Are you free to come over? I've got something I want*
> *to talk to you about.*

My phone immediately pinged in reply,

> *Sure, I'll walk over.*

❖

Chapter 14 - Coming Clean

I opened the door to a concerned look on Finn's face. I hung his coat, trying to avoid his eyes, and offered him something to drink.

"Am I gonna need a drink?" he asked, trying to catch my eye.

"No, no, it's nothing like that - I don't think," I mumbled the last part under my breath.

"Sounds like I'll take that drink. Do you have a beer?"

"Sure," I smiled, walking into my kitchen.

Once we both had beers and sat on the couch, I turned to him and said, "I've been looking into the arson of my storage locker."

"What? Maggie, what are you talking about?"

"Let me tell you the whole thing, and then you can be mad at me, but please let me tell you why first. Okay?"

I paused, waiting for a response.

"Okay."

He settled back into the couch in a listening pose and took another swig from his bottle.

"My only priority is my kids and how this could impact them; please understand that."

"Maggie, what are you talking about?"

"I researched the strip club owner in Texas, Steve Croft, who was convicted of homicide and arson. Fingerprints at that crime scene match those found in my storage locker. In one of the articles that I read about that crime, it mentioned the name of the strip club that burned, the Brass Ass. My ex's current wife worked there as a stripper but left years before the fire happened - I think."

"What? How do you-"

"Please let me tell you everything and then ask all the questions you want, okay?"

"Yeah, okay," he grimaced and made a zipping motion with his hand across his mouth.

"I wasn't sure it was the same club that Amber worked in, so I hired a private investigator in Texas…her name is MJ Barnes…and she confirmed it is the same."

"What?" he said as he choked down a mouthful of beer.

"But that connection doesn't explain why someone would want my locker burned ten years later. The only thing I could think of was all my divorce paperwork. We had a three-week trial, with depositions, live testimony, forensic accountants, private investigators, you name it - it was God awful. But it produced thousands of pages of evidence. All of these would normally be in my storage locker, but I had them in my attic here to scan and then get rid of. I started reading through it all because my memory of the trial is sketchy, and it turns out I don't remember most of it. Maybe I even blocked it out. There's a lot of money movement and lots of accounts. Plus, MJ learned more about what happened at the Brass Ass. My ex was a big spender in the VIP room - apparently, those rooms are like the dark web before it existed - you could get anything you wanted, and money flowed. I have account numbers from my divorce and some bank statements from him, and quick addition shows money movements in the millions through his accounts - way more than he should have based on his business."

I paused to catch my breath, forcing my shoulders down away from my ears.

"One other thing is the involvement of an investor named Tom. Both the Brass Ass and my ex's consulting firm had an investor named Tom. My ex said his last name was Burke and that the investor was actually Burke's cousin, but Croft couldn't remember Tom's last name. Oh, and I actually visited Steve Croft on death row in Texas to try and figure out if -"

Finn cut me off, "Whoa. Can I ask questions now?"

"One more thing - the reason I didn't tell you earlier is because I was afraid of what the impact on my children would be if I pointed the finger at my ex, even indirectly. Plus, I know how it looks when an ex-wife accuses her ex-husband, especially given how acrimonious our divorce was. I knew I needed more than just my gut feelings or my suspicions. I know I still only have the thinnest of circumstantial evidence, but the connection to the club is enough to link the two fires so I knew I had to tell you. Plus, the whole Tom coincidence is weird right?"

"I'm done waiting," said Finn. "How long have you been at this?"

"Only a couple of months - I saw Croft just before Christmas."

"I don't know what to say. You realize, Miss Associate Professor of

Criminology, that you could have compromised our case? Plus, we haven't caught the guy yet, and you could be in danger."

"That's why I'm coming to you now. All I wanted to do was look to see if there really was a link to the club. There is. Then I read some of my divorce paperwork, and there was enough in it that I stopped and called you. I know this is more than I should be doing by myself at this point."

"Really? At this point? This is a police investigation. Once you got the link to the club, you should have told me."

"I know, but I just needed to be sure. My kids will never forgive me if I'm the one to point the finger at their dad and I'm wrong. They may never forgive me even if I'm right."

"Okay, okay, I understand. But I still can't believe you went to Texas to talk to the guy. What if he's involved, and now they know you're on to them?"

My phone rang, saving me from an answer. It was Meryl checking on me now that they were all down at their dad's for New Year's. I told her I wasn't alone and that I was discussing the case with Finn.

"The case, huh?" she joked.

"Yes, it's gotten a little more complicated than we originally thought."

"How so?" she asked.

"Not sure yet, but they have new leads they're running down."

"That's good, I guess. What else are you up to?"

"I'm scanning all the divorce paperwork so I can throw away all those boxes."

"Finally. I don't know why you kept the divorce stuff for so long. It's just depressing. I thought you kept it in your storage locker, so you didn't have to see it?"

"I did, but it's time I dealt with it and got rid of it. I've got all the boxes here to go through."

"Ugh, aren't there a ton of them?" she asked.

"Yeah," Carter's voice piped up in the background. "Why not just toss them, Mom?"

"Oh, hey, Carter, I didn't realize I was on speaker. That's the plan once I get them scanned. What are you up to? Enjoying the Florida sun with your dad?"

"Sun, yes, dad, no, he's on a business trip, back the day after tomorrow."

"That's too bad, but I'm glad you're at least relaxing in the sun. Have fun and give Ruby a kiss for me. I'd better get back to Finn. I love you guys."

"Will do, love you too." And with that, she hung up. I swiveled to face Finn again.

"Okay, start at the beginning and take me through what you have in more detail. And I'm gonna need all that divorce paperwork, too," said Finn.

"We're gonna need a pizza and more beer," I ordered delivery, went to the fridge for two more beers, and talked Finn through all I had done and uncovered until the doorbell rang.

We ate our thin crust pizza and continued to talk through the evidence. I took him into my office once we finished dinner and showed him the mountains of paperwork created through my divorce.

"I told you. It's awful. I've been scanning it as I go. I could email it to you, but that's only a tiny fraction of it. I guess you better just take it all."

"Well, let's load it into your car and get it down to the station. The sooner it is out of your hands, the safer you'll be."

We boxed the loose papers and then ferried the boxes out to my car, packing until it sagged under the weight.

"I'll drop it off first thing in the morning on my way to the university. Does eight o'clock work?" I asked.

"Sure, I'll be there, and I'll get a couple of the uniformed guys to help. Maggie, please don't do this again on your own. You really could have been in danger."

"Yes, sir," I saluted and smiled. I stretched up on my toes to kiss him and then said, "Thank you for listening. I was so scared you'd be mad at me."

"I may still be mad later, but right now, I want to get you safe and figure out what is going on. I care about you, Maggie."

"You do?"

"I do."

"I care about you too - that's why all of this was so hard. I hated keeping it from you."

"Don't do it again, okay?"

"I promise I won't."

I smiled, and we kissed again, deeper and longer, this time until a chill rolled down my spine.

"I better go, or I won't."

"Don't," I said, taking his hand and leading him down the hall.

❖

Chapter 15 – Follow the Money

The screaming car alarm woke me, Finn, and Pumpkin with a jolt. Finn jumped out of bed, pulled on his pants, stuffed his feet in his shoes, and grabbed his shirt while running towards the front of the house. I grabbed my robe, shoved my feet into sneakers, and ran after him, calling Pumpkin to run as the red glow of fire out the front windows lit my living room. Pumpkin ran with me out the front door of our home as flames leaped from my car and jumped into the air. Finn yelled for me to get a hose while he dialed 911. The winter cover was on the outdoor faucet, so it took me agonizing minutes to reattach the hose and get the water flowing. When the fire truck pulled up with sirens blaring, we had just gotten a stream directed at the porch to protect the house. They cautioned us back, fearing an explosion, and trained their foam on the car.

Deja vu flooded over me as I squatted beside Pumpkin and pressed my face into her fur. I held her tight to protect her and to calm myself. Finn knelt with us, wrapped my coat around me, hugged me, and kissed my head. Neighbors had started to arrive to watch the firefighters work and marvel at the strength of the fire against their efforts. Megan appeared and hugged me tight, reminding me that Pumpkin and I were safe, and that's all that mattered.

Then she noticed Finn, who had gone over to speak to the firefighters and hugged me again, whispering, "Good for you."

I wept into her neck as she hugged me, releasing the fear I had been holding. Once I calmed down, I pulled myself together, smoothing my hair and pulling my coat around me, and walked out to my neighbors still milling in the street and thanked them for their concern. Pumpkin stood sentry by me, her head barely leaving my right thigh. Megan collected Pumpkin and me, shivering, and shepherded us back into my home. We stood looking out the front window as the remnants of my car still smoked and the firefighters loitered in my driveway ensuring it didn't re-ignite.

"What happened?" she finally asked.

"I don't know; we woke up to the car alarm and flames. I don't know what's going on. I'm frightened."

She put her arm around my waist and squeezed me to her. "Well, tonight you and Pumpkin should come stay with me. Get a good night's sleep, and we'll figure this out tomorrow."

"Thank you, but I don't want to leave my home. I just found it - the first real home I've had in decades. I won't let this scare me away."

"But maybe you should be scared away?" she asked with concern.

"No, assuming this wasn't an accident, they could have burned the house and didn't; I really think we're okay."

"If you say so, but do you understand why this happened? If not, can you be sure they won't return?"

"No, I don't understand this, but I'm working on it."

"Just be careful, okay? And if you change your mind, I've got a warm bed right down the street; knock."

"Okay, I promise." I finally smiled a little. We remained standing at the window. Friends wrapped in each other's arms and Pumpkin at attention by my side.

When the last remnants of the fire had been doused, only the frame of my car remained. The fire chief reported that an accelerant had been used. Everything that had been in my car was gone. Dawn was breaking, and my neighbors returned to their warm homes once the excitement was over. Megan offered to stay, but I knew she had a long day ahead of her, so I sent her home, promising to catch up that afternoon. When the fire truck finally pulled away, and the police statements were completed, Finn and I remained, drained and deflated.

"I'm sorry," said Finn, "this is all my fault."

"What are you talking about? I'm your alibi for the fire; I know you didn't do it," I quipped, trying to smile.

"I should have taken the files to the station immediately, not left them in your car overnight."

"Someone is watching me, Finn. They must have seen us loading the car. I'm glad the files weren't still in the house, or God only knows what could have happened."

"But how did they know to watch you? The Texas arson and death were a decade ago. Your storage locker burned months ago," he said and then paused. "You were on speaker phone to your kids."

"Yeah, but they said Ted was out of town."

"Where was Amber?" His question hung in the air between us. "Could she have heard and told Ted?"

"I guess so. But how would we prove that? And now we've lost any proof we might have had in the divorce paperwork," I sighed, looking at Finn for hope.

He didn't offer any, adding, "No way court records are kept fifteen years or even that your lawyer kept them all that long."

"Agreed, but we've got an ace in the hole."

"Oh yeah, what's that?" he asked, taking his turn at hope.

"Not what, who. MJ Barnes. I sent her the financials to review by email, and there's a copy. Plus, much of the paperwork was emailed to me and by me over the years. I'll still have a lot of digital copies I can pull together."

Finn hugged me. "Thank God for MJ and email then. Can't wait to meet her; she sounds quite a character."

"She is; you'll love her."

"I guess I should get ready and get into the station. Can I use your shower?"

"Only if you don't mind sharing," I said with a grin.

Later, Finn and I walked to his house, where he quickly changed and drove me to the university to teach for the day. I exited his car and said, "It feels like deja vu."

"Except this was a mistake. Now we know what they wanted in the first fire up here and maybe even in Texas a decade ago. We'll get them."

"We?" I asked.

"Not that 'we," he said with a wink. "Take care today, Maggie. I'll be back to pick you up at five." And he drove away.

I followed my morning routine of coffee from the cafeteria and class preparation but my mind was a million miles away, pondering the fire and what could be in those files that was so important. I forwarded all the files I could find quickly in my emails over the years to Finn with a fingers-crossed emoji, promising to send a more comprehensive package later, and then tried to focus on my lecture for the day.

When it was time for my class, I went to the bathroom and splashed water on my face. "You can do this, Maggie; stay present," I said to my reflection, and then walked down the hall and into my classroom.

I began my planned curriculum on the drivers of gang violence in inner cities and law enforcement response. About five minutes into my lecture, I stopped and said, "This is important, and we will return to it, but I want to try something different today. Let's do a case study."

The class, attentively taking notes, now sat up straighter and listened differently. One voice from the back called out, "Cool!"

I smiled and continued, "I am going to give you a scenario, and I want you to posit the potential drivers of the behavior - the motives of the criminals, whether sociological or psychological - nothing is out of bounds. Got it?"

Many heads bobbed in unison, and the students leaned forward as I began.

"There are three crimes seemingly unconnected - we need to determine the *mens rea* - the guilty mind at work behind them all.

"Crime #1 - Ten years ago, a strip club in Dallas, Texas, burned to the ground. An accelerant was used. One of the entertainers is killed in the fire, but it was after hours, so she shouldn't have been there. The owner of the club is prosecuted on the theory of arson for insurance proceeds and convicted of felony murder. He is currently on death row.

"Crime # 2 - Three months ago, a storage facility in Connecticut was burned. Only one lock on one unit had been cut before the fire. There were no injuries, but the locker, as well as others around it, was destroyed. The locker's owner, a woman, reported only memorabilia in the locker. Fingerprints at the scene were linked to the Texas fire ten years ago. No other links between the crimes were found. There were no injuries.

"Crime #3 - Last night, the same woman's car was burned, and it contained all her divorce files from fifteen years prior. As in each of the other fires, the presence of an accelerant was confirmed. There were no injuries."

I paused while the students finished their notes on the facts, and then I continued, "Three details seemingly link the crimes. First, a fingerprint links the Texas fire to the storage locker fire. Second, her ex-husband, whom she divorced fifteen years ago, is now married to a former entertainer from that strip club in Texas. However, that dancer left the club at least six years before the fire. And third, her ex-husband's company and the club both have an investor named Tom."

"Let's hear it," I finally asked, "what's going on here?"

Hands flew up. Liam was in the front row, so I began with him. "It's gotta be linked to the paperwork that burned in her car, right? Something in the divorce?"

'Yeah, but how does that explain the strip club fire?" I challenged. 'That crime was over a decade ago."

'Follow the money!" shouted Josie. She hardly ever spoke up, so the rest of the class turned in shock at her outcry.

'Okay, Josie, let's hear it - tell us why," I said, encouraging her.

'It's the greatest motivator. A divorce is always about money. Strip clubs are rolling in it, and there is lots of cash. The first fire doesn't tell us much, but the third one tells us everything. It tells us the motive. The divorce paperwork. We can't know the exact motive without knowing what was in that paperwork, but I'd bet it'll be in the general category of money."

All other hands dropped, and the class continued to stare at her.

"Okay," I said. "Let's start there. What could happen at a strip club years after an entertainer worked there that would end up in a husband's divorce paperwork even more years later?"

Liam returned to the conversation, "What if it's not about the stripper at the club? What if it's about the husband?"

"What do you mean, Liam? Keep going," I prodded.

"Well, aren't we assuming he stopped attending the club when she quit? But what if he didn't? After all, he married a stripper. What if he hung out at the club long before he met her and maybe even long after?"

Josie added, "and got involved in some shady financial dealings at the club, which somehow made it into his divorce paperwork. That could also explain the mystery investor named Tom, couldn't it?"

"But why didn't any of this get caught in the divorce if it's all in the paperwork?" asked Liam, turning from Josie back to me.

I jumped in, saying, "Well, it could just be the lawyers' sloppiness, but it could also be that they weren't looking at the numbers that way. In a divorce, you're just focused on dividing assets and looking for one spouse to spend away marital assets; it's called dissipation. You aren't looking for other kinds of money movement."

"So, we think that somewhere, buried in all the divorce paperwork, is a detail that will link all three crimes, including that Tom guy?" summarized Liam.

"Yep," said Josie confidently. "It has to, or they never would have torched the storage locker and car. After all, if this theory is right, whoever killed the stripper in that arson in Texas has gotten away with it for ten years. Coming out of hiding to burn everything potentially opens it all back up. It's hazardous. The pros of doing so must have outweighed the cons."

"Shazam!" shouted another student just as the bell rang, signaling the end of class. Usually, all the students jumped from their seats at the bell, but this time, they all sat, waiting for more.

"Y'all liked the case study?" I asked, to nods and shouts of "yeah" from around the room. "Okay, we'll pick up on this next class. It got you all thinking like detectives, but I want us to go deeper as criminologists. What drove the criminals in this case? What would the attributes and behaviors of the criminals be? Your assignment is to think that over and come prepared to discuss. See you Wednesday." And the class filed out.

I sat quietly, rolling their comments over in my mind. Josie had echoed what Ted's office manager, Liz, had told me years earlier, "follow the money." But her summary also clarified things for me. There really must be something in that now-burned paperwork. I just had to hope it was in the part I had scanned and sent to MJ or found among my emails over the years.

I retreated to my office and spent the rest of the afternoon on the phone with the insurance adjusters, scrolling through car lot ads to find a good deal. Just before five, I packed up my laptop, grabbed my purse, and walked out to meet Finn. He pulled up with a quick honk and a big grin. I climbed into his Jeep, tucking my bags at my feet, and leaned over for a quick peck.

As I did, he leaned forward, extended the kiss, and hugged me firmly, asking, "How are you doing?"

"I'm okay. I think I'm moving through the stages of grief and now am angry. Talking to the insurance adjusters could have brought it on, but I think it's just that some jerk keeps burning everything I love. I've had that car for eight years. She was great."

"She?" asked Finn, a smile curling at the edges of his mouth.

"Yes, she. I spent part of this afternoon trying to find a replacement. I'll have to go to New Haven for a good deal."

"Can I take you? We could go this weekend."

"That would be great. And could I ask another favor? Could you drive me to the rental car place on Route 32? My insurance will pay a loaner until I buy a new car."

"I don't mind being your chauffeur this week."

"I know you don't, and that's so sweet, but insurance covers it, and you're busy. I'd feel better with my own car."

"I get it, no problem."

Once I got sorted into a rented sedan, Finn followed me home. Happy to be back, I let Pumpkin relieve herself outside and then fed her. Once she was sorted out, I grabbed a bottle of red wine and pulled out some assorted cheeses, sliced meats, and crackers.

"Dinner?" I smiled and laid the tray on the living room coffee table as Pumpkin sniffed the air and trailed behind me. Finn poured the wine, and I fell back into the deep corner of the sofa. Having already inhaled her dinner, Pumpkin curled on the floor between us, hoping for crumbs.

"How are you doing?" Finn asked again.

"I'm angry but exhausted at the same time. I need this to end. I'm scared, and I don't like that feeling."

Finn lifted my legs across his lap as I shifted to face him.

"I spent the day going through the files you sent. There's a lot there, so I contacted a buddy I know down in the city who works these kinds of cases. He said he could go through them but needed a week. In the meantime, I would feel better if you and Pumpkin stayed at my place."

"No, please, I won't let them drive me out of the only home I have had in years. Plus, don't they think it's over? That they burned it all?"

"Okay then, not to be presumptuous, and I am happy to sleep on the couch, but I'd like to stay here with you, just to be safe - until this is sorted out."

"No need for the couch," I smiled and raised my glass.

❖

Chapter 16 – The Details

I woke at 4 am with sleep still clinging to my eyes but a desire to get up and start pouring over the divorce financials. As I pulled up the files, a text popped up from MJ.

> *Up and at 'em this morning! I'm sure we'll find what we need in what you sent over.*

I responded,

> *You don't have to help; you've done enough, and I can't afford much more of your time ⋯.*

> *And another thing – someone burned my car last night – a Molotov cocktail apparently – all my divorce files were in it! Thank God I sent so much to you already! Plus, I have emailed bits and pieces over the years, and I pulled some of those together to try and recreate as much as I can of what was lost. I already sent Finn a small batch but there's a lot more to collect.*

She typed,

> *WTF?!? I'm taking this personally now; today is on me. We'll get the bastard!*

I sighed, texting back,

> *I barely know you; I can't thank you enough. I'll let the Yale law team know you're helping – maybe they*

have some budget.

She finished the chat, writing,

> *We girls gotta stick together. As soon as I have anything, I'll text ⋯*

With MJ as inspiration, I began to read. The numbers danced before me until Finn roused at six.

"Morning, sunshine," I called.

"Wow, how long have you been up?" Finn muttered as he shuffled into the kitchen. I poured him coffee to give him a moment to acclimate to my energy before I began to share.

"Been up a while - can I run something by you?"

"On a sip of coffee, I'm not sure what kind of sounding board I'll be, but give me a try."

"I've been over the numbers now, and during my divorce trial, I even had forensic accountants review them and testify. If there was something in the numbers themselves, we, the accountants, would have caught it. Don't you think?"

"I guess so, but that's our only lead and seems to be what they were targeting."

"Not necessarily. There are more than numbers in account statements. There are words, names, and dates. Ted testified more about the dates and events during our trial than specific numbers. He even testified that he couldn't remember who loaned him $100,000 to start his business. It didn't matter to the divorce at the time, so no one pursued it."

"Sorry, he said he didn't remember who loaned him 100 grand unde oath, and no one pursued it?"

"Nope. Don't get me started on my divorce lawyer - a different story for a different day, and it may need to involve tequila," I said with smirk.

"Got it," Finn said through a grin as he pulled out a chair and sa across from me.

"So, I'm thinking, what if it's not the amount of money, which wa the focus of my divorce, but the source of the money? Or the movement of the money? Or the names on the accounts? Or some combination of all of those things? What if they are afraid that it is in the records somewhere?"

Before Finn could respond, I kept going, "There were a couple of big sums that Ted spent at the Brass Ass, and he was questioned about in the depositions and a little even at trial. The one I remember i $10,000 in one night."

"Wow, I can see why you remember that."

"No, you don't. It wasn't the amount. I mean, it was, but it was more because he spent it on our 10th wedding anniversary. I found that ou during the trial. He thought it was funny."

"Ugh. Sorry."

"Yep, me too, he wasn't - they asked him that too."

"Ouch."

"Anyways," I said, rolling my eyes, "he wouldn't answer what it was for, he said, and this isn't a joke, 'you were in the army, use your imagination,' to my lawyer."

"And everyone let that go, even the judge?" Finn asked, shaking his head.

"Like I said, another long story for another day, but the short answer is that we were divorced in Florida - a real old boys club in the divorce court. Anyhow, what I was thinking about this morning was, what if the issue was what the money was for, linked to, or something else about money moving through the club?"

"Not bad, Agatha Christie. Any ideas?" he said, lifting his steaming mug and taking a large swallow.

"Well, during the divorce, one of my distant cousins reached out to share his support for me and the kids, and when I mentioned the strip clubs and the money Teddy had spent, he said it had to be drugs. Before you ask, I didn't ask how he knew that. He said at strip clubs; you can charge anything you want - drugs, guns, women, and the club charges it back as one line item on your bill, as if it is all just entertainment for the night."

"Yeah, I've heard of that," he smiled. "Even at bachelor parties, and all that can happen, you only get one charge."

"But is tax fraud worth killing and two more arsons over a decade later if everyone does it? Doesn't it have to be something more? That's why I think it must be about the accounts and the other information linked to each," I added.

"I'm starting to warm to your theory. That or the coffee is kicking in," Finn smiled.

"I only have an afternoon class today, so I will go back over the account files and any other records I have attached to emails over the years to try and pull everything I've got on the accounts. As soon as I've got it pieced together, I'll send the file to you and MJ."

"She's still on this?"

"Yep, she texted this morning, and there is no charge for today. She's amazing. I'll ask the Yale team if they can cover her costs."

"What does the Yale team think of all of this?" he asked.

"I think I amuse them, to be honest. They are a law school clinic that focuses on capital punishment. That means they only take on death penalty cases and are very selective in those they choose. They told me that they selected Croft's case for appeal because it's in Texas, where the death penalty is imposed more often than in any other state, and because his conviction was purely circumstantial. That said, I'm not sure they have much hope of an actual vindication for him. So, they support me as long as I don't make things worse for him. That's why they're keeping some distance from my investigation, and I hope they'll cover at least some of MJ's fees."

"I do have to meet her then to thank her," Finn said as he pulled himself to his feet and wandered back to the bedroom. He emerged a few minutes later dressed and hair still askew. He tucked his shirt into his jeans and then ran his hand through his hair as he pulled on his coat.

"I'll call you later," he said and bent to kiss me on the forehead.

I kissed him properly and said, "Thanks, Finn. For everything."

"You got it, Maggie," he said, winking at me as he turned and left.

I spent the rest of the morning combing through years of emails with attachments to pull out every detail on the accounts. I had an electronic file full of everything I could find by lunch. I was pleased it had more than just financials; it included Ted and Amber's depositions, the evidence Ted's office manager Liz had shared with me, and the trial transcript. I zipped the file and sent it to Finn and MJ before jumping in the shower to prepare for work.

❖

Chapter 17 – The Case Study

"Okay, class, let's start where we left off. I think we agreed that Josie and Liam were on to something last class about the money trail. But your assignment was to come prepared to discuss the *mens rea* and behaviors of the criminals in this case. Thoughts?"

Hands popped up across the room. I picked a student sitting in the middle of the group, "Carrie, why don't you start us off?"

"Well, I was thinking about the profile of an arsonist. Generally male, young, and a serial offender. He probably has petty crimes on his record dating back to adolescence."

"Good, Carrie, but let me challenge you on the traditional profile. That profile says the attacks are generally random unless motivated by specific revenge or anger. Do you think we have that here, given some of the links we have established?"

Carrie furrowed her brow, "No, I guess not. This arsonist doesn't fit the normal profile of random fires, and we haven't established a revenge or anger angle either."

"What does make sense then? Why arson? Other ideas?"

There was a pause, and then Liam quietly said, "What about an amateur trying to either destroy or cover evidence? We've all seen enough movies to know it might be something someone would think of."

"Keep going, Liam," I encouraged. "How does that apply to all three crimes?"

'Well, I understand it better for the last two. They feel all about destroying evidence. The first has me stumped because I think the fire, in that case, could mean three different things. Either it was to cover the murder of the stripper, to murder the stripper, or to burn something in the club, and the stripper was collateral damage. Or, I guess, it could be some combination."

Agreement from all around the room filled the quiet when he finished speaking.

I asked, "Do the last two fires point to one or more of those scenarios being more likely than the others?"

Josie picked up the thought, saying, "The last two arsons feel like the first one missed something in the fire. This makes me think a big part of the first crime was the fire, not the homicide. What was the cause of death of the victim?"

"Tiffany Schmidt was her name," I said. "Cause of death was blunt force trauma to the head. However, she could have simply fallen trying to escape the fire. The medical examiner could not tell what caused the injury."

"What do we know about her?" asked Kipp from the back row.

"That's a good question, Kipp, not much. The articles I've read say other dancers came forward after the fire to identify her. That tells me she didn't have family, or at least that no family came forward. The owner of the club, Croft, described her as a nobody and potentially a drug addict. So does that indicate more in our profile?"

"Maybe it points to her being collateral damage rather than a target?"

added Liam.

"So that would have us continue to focus on the money trail and not a specific motive linked to the victim of the fire. We'll focus on the cover-up angle. Does that sound right to everyone?" I prodded. "And eventually, we also need to explain the ten-year gap between the first crime and the second and third."

Nods and murmurs of "yeah" echoed around the room. I followed up by asking, "So this is about the money trail that began ten years ago in the strip club. Then the latest arsons are part of an ongoing cover up - either a continuing effort to burn what was missed or it could be a continuing cover-up to make sure the homicide stays solved with Croft as a patsy. Is that what we're thinking?"

More nods.

"So, how do we figure out which it is?"

Silence.

"Let me float an idea," I added. "One element found in pattern crimes is that at the beginning of the pattern, the criminals are not as good at crime as they later become. Detectives often look way back into a criminal's past to find errors they made early on. Perhaps that could be the link in the documentation that goes back fifteen years to the divorce. Maybe the criminals know that an early mistake is captured in the divorce paperwork?"

"So, we need to read the divorce files to find the mistake they think it captures?" asked Josie.

"But it was burned," said Liam.

"Not all of it," I added. "The police have some. The hope is that it will be enough."

The bell rang, and no one moved.

"What's our next step?" asked Josie.

"I can ask the police if we could help read the paperwork as a class project. I don't know if they'll allow it, but I can try."

"Cool," said Liam, and the rest of the class echoed his sentiment as they filed out past me.

❖

Chapter 18 – Needle In a Spreadsheet

"Absolutely not," said Finn after I had called to relay the request to help. "You've already potentially compromised our case with your sleuthing; involving your class wouldn't help the situation."

"But we'd have all the additional eyes to read all the paperwork. Could we maybe help by reading at your direction and looking for things you ask for us to search for in the documents? Like account numbers, dates, names, or amounts?"

"I don't know, Maggie. I know how much you want to help move the investigation along, but we have to be careful because you're the victim. Let me ask the chief. Let me see what I can do, okay?"

"Okay, Finn, I understand, of course. I just have an eager class of students I'm trying to involve if possible. They're learning so much more through case studies than dry lectures. But I totally understand the position you're in. Thanks for considering our offer."

"Of course, Maggie. I'll call you later."

And with that, Finn disconnected.

I got myself a cup of lemon verbena tea, grabbed my iPad, and padded over to my couch to continue reading through the digital breadcrumbs left by my ex. I figured it had to be some combination of names, dates, and amounts that was making whoever was burning everything nervous. Maybe if I figured out the what, it would lead me to the who. But I didn't even know where to start. One thing I had never understood was how Ted had funded his secret life. Everything I had learned about his life away from me was that it was lavish - fancy hotels, gourmet meals, lots of strip clubs, and a high-maintenance girlfriend he kept in an apartment, which he furnished with everything they might want or need.

All I knew about our finances was that he made a good salary but nothing that would support that kind of spending. We were comfortable but had a budget. Even as I thought it, I chastised myself for believing I had known what our finances were. But still, the gap in spending was enormous. Maybe that was something….

I pulled up the documents his office manager, Liz, had shared. I remembered the adage that criminals made their biggest mistakes early before they learned better. Maybe these early documents Liz had collected would catch an error. The most obvious thing was the check that Ted had handwritten to himself for $20,000 in early 2005. There weren't any other checks handwritten like that, at least not that Liz had mentioned or provided. Maybe the fact that there was only one check like that meant that he recognized his mistake. So, what was the possible issue with the check?

I printed out a hard copy to examine. It was a business check, and he was the co-owner, so there was no issue with him writing a check. It was handwritten to him by him, not to cash. The check didn't seem to offer any leads. Until I flipped it over, the signature was his name but not in his hand. It was a passable forgery and obviously had navigated bank scrutiny, but I would know his handwriting anywhere, and this was too neat. We had a joke that he could have been a doctor with his handwriting, but this signature was legible. The front was handwritten by him, but the back was endorsed as him by someone else. Plus, there were a lot of notations by the bank, more than usual. Was this something? Theft? Or was the issue that he made it out to himself? Why do that? Why not just make the check out to cash if he wanted money?

I continued to pour through the Liz file, as I affectionately named it, finding credit card statements marked up for reimbursement in Ted's handwriting, printed checks made out to himself for thousands of dollars, dozens of strip club receipts with the code word "DEV" written across them, which I assumed meant "development," a spreadsheet labeled "Endeavor Sex Expenses," emails, and finally the *Dear Amy* column Liz had mentioned when we met for lunch. I went through all of it again, cross-checking dates and amounts.

As I sifted through the digital pile of documents, I remembered during the divorce trial when my lawyer had produced the check for $20,000 and shown it to Ted. The smug satisfaction he had displayed since day one had briefly fallen to reveal surprise before his mask quickly resumed. It was the only financial evidence we used at trial that they had not produced to us. We had found it on our own.

My lawyer had not used anything else in Liz's file, but Ted must have wondered what else we had. His lawyer had jumped to her feet, objecting and protesting loudly to the judge that it must have been illegally obtained. Her argument failed as they obviously should have produced it for us as part of discovery.

When it was my turn to testify, his lawyer had wasted no time going right to that point, probing where I had gotten the check and what else I had. My lawyer had stopped her onslaught with his own objections, and my source was never revealed. They also never got an answer as to what else I had.

But now I wondered. Everything we had for trial was documents Ted and his lawyer had given to us. Those documents were what my accountants and lawyers had reviewed.

So, from Ted's perspective, all of those must have been fine to share with us. The only documents we had that had not been provided by Ted were those I had gotten from Liz. So maybe those were the issues? Maybe not knowing what else I had gotten from Liz was causing the arsonist to act?

I called Finn and walked him through my hypothesis. He must have thought it had some merit because, at first, he was quiet and then said he'd be right over. When he arrived, I offered him something to drink, but he waved off the suggestion, asking me to walk him through the Liz file and all I understood it to mean.

When I was done sharing my analysis, Finn took me up on a glass of water, and we both sat staring at the documents I had printed.

"I hate to say this to his wife at the time," started Finn. "The sex club spending is gross but nothing to commit crimes over. The thing that is interesting is those four or five checks involving his private banker that Liz gave to you. He seems to take money from the business account and move it to another account at the same bank. The notations by the banker on the checks themselves of his driver's license verification are detailed and seem to indicate some reluctance or at least ass-covering on her part."

"I saw that too, but I don't know whose name is on that other account. We never got any information on that one"

"It wasn't yours or your family's, at least? You don't recognize the number?"

"No, I checked that for the trial. None of the accounts at that bank had anything to do with me. We assumed they were all business accounts."

"Okay, well, that's a start. The amounts are round numbers and…" he paused, pulling out his phone's calendar and typing and referencing the checks before continuing, "many of the checks were written over a weekend."

"What's the problem with that?"

"Those are both red flags for money laundering. If you add in the movement between accounts, that's a third warning flag. And if the banker was checking ID, then the movement between accounts wasn't between identical account owners. They were checking ID because the account owner was changing, and they needed Ted, whose name was on the first account, to authorize the movement."

"Why would he be laundering money from a consulting business?"

"He wouldn't be. But maybe he is doing it for someone else or another business, and maybe the strip club was part of it all. Remember I mentioned a buddy down in the city that I shared your files with?" I nodded as he continued, "Well, he's part of OCCB."

Seeing my expression, he explained, "Organized Crime Control Bureau - they're the NYPD experts on this stuff. I'll go to him with this additional information and see what he can make of it. Okay?"

"No names, though, right? I don't want to start anything yet if we don't have to."

"Not yet, no. I'll say it's just a hypothetical. Okay? Plus, none of this is their jurisdiction anyway."

I exhaled, "Okay."

"I'll take these copies and go see him. I'd rather talk this through face to face. I'll call you on my way back."

"Ugh. I'm going to be on pins and needles. Hurry, please."

"Like the wind," he said, and with a wink and a quick kiss on the cheek, he gathered all the papers and left.

Before he was out of the driveway, Megan was on her way over. We knew it would be late before we heard from Finn, but by the time my phone buzzed, we had both fallen asleep on my couch with Pumpkin wedged between us.

I jolted awake, answering, "Hello?"

"On my way back - did I wake you?" Finn asked.

I pulled my phone away from my ear to check the time. 12:17.

"We must have fallen asleep."

"We?"

"Megan, Pumpkin, and me."

"It'll be too late by the time I get back tonight to go through everything he said, but we have a rough idea of what could have been happening. Why don't we meet tomorrow at noon for lunch at Dog Lane Cafe?"

"Okay, we'll see you then. This 'we' is only Megan and me this time," I said with a smile, hanging up and then rousing Megan, sharing the plan and sending her home for a good night's sleep.

❖

Chapter 19 – The Trigger

Megan and I were early, getting a booth in the back for privacy. We ordered iced teas and were unusually quiet waiting on Finn. I strummed my fingers on the linoleum-topped table until Megan reached across to silence them.

"He'll be here," she said. "We're early."

"I know, I know. I've never been good at patience," I responded with a shrug by way of explanation.

Just after noon, he strode into the cafe, and I waved to catch his attention. As he sat, the server appeared again, and we each chose quickly, anxious to finish the business of ordering so we could talk.

"Well?" I said, poorly concealing my impatience once the server had left us.

Finn smiled and pulled out his notepad from the file he had laid on the booth next to him.

"My buddy said it's all pretty straightforward as to what they could have been doing. Although, admittedly, we don't have proof."

"And?" Megan prodded, casting me a side-eyed glance of support.

"Hold your horses, I'll get it out. There are two angles, and he says it could have been either or both. He gave me a disclaimer that this is all speculation, but I said we'd take it anyway. The first angle is the checks to himself for big, round dollar amounts. Those could be embezzlement or him siphoning off kickbacks he was getting from the strip club."

"Kickbacks for what?" I interrupted.

"Let me get through it, Maggie, okay?" Finn said, furrowing his brows in concentration as he scanned his notes.

I nodded, drawing my fingers across my lips and miming the turn of a key.

"So, Ryan, my buddy, says that strip clubs invoice in a single line item for the entire amount spent in a night at the club."

"Yeah, we saw that on his credit card statements," I blurted.

His look quieted me again, and Megan grabbed my hand, squeezing in solidarity.

"Well, because they invoice that way, there is no breakdown of what the amount was for - like you would see on a restaurant bill, for example. You know, at a restaurant, your bill would show a hamburger, soda, and dessert, which would then be added with tax for your total. But at a strip club, you just get the total, and there is no breakdown," Finn paused for a breath, and Megan squeezed my hand again, encouraging patience.

"That means the club could also overcharge, and there would be no way to check against what was actually purchased," he continued. "Because Ted's bills were paid by his company and not him personally, all overcharges would get paid for by his firm. This could all link to those checks he was writing to himself if the club was overcharging as part of an agreement with Ted. Because he is the business owner, he would pay the inflated bills on a corporate credit card, and then he might have been splitting the overcharges with the club. In effect, the club was helping Ted launder money by overcharging his firm and then kicking back the profit to him personally while taking a cut for themselves. Plus, his business was recording all the strip club spending as business development and writing it all off on their taxes. It was a win-win-win. Those checks you got your hands on might be Ted moving the kickbacks around. It would explain the unknown income source."

"But why would he put the ill-gotten money back in corporate accounts?" I blurted, unable to help myself.

"Aha," smiled Finn.

"That's the second piece Ryan brought up. He said that this scam was easy to pull and nearly impossible for the IRS to police, so he doesn't think Ted was the only club customer involved. If Ted could do this, so could a lot of other small business owners. He also said that given the amounts moving through Ted's accounts against the credit card statements you saw, which showed far less in his own spending at the club than what was showing up in his accounts, he might have been a middleman for the scheme. He could have been recruiting other small business owners into the money laundering through kick-back business. That would bring him a cut of everyone's money he brought in. That, apparently, would be big bucks. Then those company checks to himself could have been a couple of different things - him moving money so his partner wouldn't get suspicious if he wasn't cut in on the deal or if he was cut in and the laundering was a big part of their own business, then it was Ted pulling his cut out at different times. My bet is that the partner was in on it because Liz's information included a lot of huge strip club receipts signed by the partner, too.

Ryan said they may have deposited some of the ill-gotten gains to their corporate accounts and reported them as consulting fees to hide what their firm was actually doing and keep up the appearance of a successful, legitimate business."

Before I could ask one of the dozens of questions queuing in my mind, our server re-appeared and placed our lunches before us. We thanked her in unison and then paused while she walked away.

"Let me get this straight," I started. "Ted didn't really have a consulting business but was a money launderer and fraudster?"

"No, not necessarily," countered Finn. "It probably didn't start that way, but it may have become that over time as he figured out and perfected the scheme. More likely is that over time, the consulting firm became a front for his real business - which was much more profitable and illegal."

Megan kept my hand in hers and said, "Oh my God, this is like the movies. But what does all this have to do with the fires? I mean, how is this relevant? Why the fires? And why is there a ten-year gap from the first in Texas to now? And how is this all tied to Maggie?"

"All of those questions have to be answered, Megan. I have a theory - at least about the first fire. Maggie, you'll have to help tie together the rest," said Finn.

"Okay," I muttered. "But I'm not sure I know."

"Let's talk it through," encouraged Megan. "Finn, what's your theory on the first fire?"

"The theory they convicted Croft under was insurance fraud - burning his business down for the insurance money. But that means the purpose of the fire was to burn down the building. Usually, folks do that because they're in debt and need the money. But I couldn't find anything online or from the Croft trial that indicated debt related to the Brass Ass. Quite the opposite, in fact. Everything we have found out sounds like there was a lot of money moving through that club. Not money on the books, but that building was still worth a lot more standing to them than burnt down. Without it, they can't launder the money. So, that means the purpose of the fire was not to burn the building but was tied to the death of Tiffany Schmidt. We know she died from a blow to the head, so the fire may have been only to cover up a murder. When you look at it that way, there's a whole new group of suspects."

"But why wouldn't Croft have said this in his defense? He was on trial for his life," asked Megan.

"Money laundering is no minor crime. The sentence is twenty years. Plus, who knows who they're in business with? He might have been scared. Remember, he has a family," explained Finn. "Or maybe Croft wasn't part of the money laundering and really didn't know anything about it."

"That makes sense based on what he told me," I added. "He said that Tom ran the VIP room; he wasn't really part of it. He got a cut for providing the room and security. It was also pretty clear when we spoke that he was scared of Tom."

"So that focuses us back on the money launderers and the likelihood that Tiffany either saw something or threatened them in some way, and they killed her for it," summarized Finn.

"Yeah, when you factor in all the shenanigans going on at that club, if Tiffany threatened blackmail or got in over her head with the wrong people, maybe she was a liability they couldn't afford," added Megan.

"Croft told me that Tiffany was sick a lot, and he assumed she was addicted to heroin. That can make people desperate for money - maybe she tried to get it from the wrong person," I added.

"Okay," said Finn. "We've got a junkie who needed money, working in a place swimming in it. She ends up dead. We may never know exactly what happened, but I think we can assume she went to the wrong person for a cut. Then we're saying the fire was to cover her killing. But I still don't see the motive for anyone involved in the money laundering to start the fire - they needed the club. If it was me and I had killed her in a moment of rage, I would have moved the body to save the club. Especially if I killed her in order to save the whole scheme as my income source."

"Seems you've really thought through a murder," I said with a wink. "But you're assuming rationale thought by the killer. Let's step into their shoes. They have just killed someone. If there had been a struggle, there could have been a lot of forensic evidence left behind. Head wounds bleed a lot. It may not have been as calculated as you have laid it out. In fact, the death by a blow to the head indicates a lack of premeditation - it sounds like the killer picked something up and struck her. Like you said, in a moment of rage. That rage clouds judgment, and before they thought it through, they could have burned down the club, which was also their golden goose."

Megan smiled, waving her arms in the air, while saying, "There's my criminologist friend! Whoop!"

Finn laughed, "I agree. "I think we have a solid theory for the killing and fire in Dallas. But why the focus on you a decade later? Remember, the fingerprints match. What was the trigger to bring the killer back out into the open? It's quite a risk to re-emerge when they'd already gotten away with a murder. Plus, this isn't a hardened criminal we're dealing with because the prints aren't in the system."

"Why does the lack of prints in the system indicate anything?" asked Megan. "Couldn't they just have gotten away with crimes all along? I mean, you just said they had gotten away with murder for a decade."

Finn and I both jumped in.

"No," we said simultaneously, looking at each other with a surprised smile.

"Go ahead, Maggie, tell her," said Finn.

"It's really unusual, almost unheard of, for criminals to get away with a pattern of criminal behavior their whole lives. The exception, tragic as it is, is pedophiles. They typically have upwards of two hundred victims by the time one of the children is brave enough to come forward and report their predator to the police. The nature of that crime actually shields the perpetrator because of the manipulation and grooming involved. But that's a topic for another day," I said with a head shake.

"For this type of crime, murder, and arson, the offender likely has many other crimes that have built to these acts. The typical offender begins with smaller crimes, like small fires, stealing cars, shoplifting, and graffiti. And because they're young, if caught, the system is lenient, and they are quickly released. But there is the beginning of a trail, a criminal record. We usually see at least a juvenile record as they learned how to commit crimes when we see serious offenses later in life – like arson or murder. Fingerprints would pull that full criminal history up.

"When these offenders are young, they test what they can get away with and then grow in confidence as their crimes grow with them. The chance of them going undetected for their whole life is highly unusual. The only explanation we sometimes see for a criminal getting away with a number of crimes for a longer period of time is that they are arrested for an unrelated crime and locked up. The original string of crimes is never tied to them because the evidence collected at those scenes didn't link them directly to the later crime scenes. But, like I said, that's rare with the advances in forensic science over the last two decades. In this case, however, because we have prints to link the crimes across the years, there has to be another explanation. If the perpetrator of the Texas fire had been arrested for anything else in the last ten years, that original fingerprint would have linked the crimes. But no link has ever been made to that print. These prints seem to indicate that this offender has never been in the system. If he had been, his prints at the time of his incarceration would have pointed to the Texas murder."

"Geez," said Megan with a long exhale. "So where does that leave us?"

I distractedly dragged a french fry through my mustard while Megan and Finn also paused to eat. We sat, chewing, for several minutes until Finn refocused us.

'I think the theory of the Dallas killing and fire is solid - even if we don't know who did it. Let's focus on our Connecticut cases and what triggered the re-emergence of this killer and arsonist after a decade. What made him or her focus on you, Maggie?"

"I've been racking my brain about that because I don't talk to my ex, and I'm not sure I have ever actually spoken to his wife, the former stripper."

"But how do you arrange the kids' visits?" asked Megan.

"Email. Texts. Or the kids do it themselves; they're older now," I answered.

"Focus on September and early October, just before the storage locker fire," encouraged Finn. "Any communication with him then?"

"Not directly. Although I did upset him and Amber by posting on her Instagram. She blocked me after that. Not that it's something I was planning to repeat."

"Maybe that's it," said Megan, leaning forward. "What was it about?"

"She was gushing over a trip to the Maldives with him and talked about how long they had been together and how great their love story was. I couldn't help myself when I saw how long she said they were an item - it pre-dated what I knew about their affair by years. It meant they started while I was pregnant with my youngest, Meryl. The timeline even differed from what they said in their depositions and under oath in court. It really upset me, so I posted that she was a stripper and he was an adulterer and cheater and that I had the documentation to prove it."

"That could be it," said Finn. "Do you know exactly what you said?"

A look of concern crossed his face.

"No. She deleted it after I posted it and then blocked me from all her accounts. But I know I said she was a stripper at the Brass Ass, and could prove it."

"Okay. Was this a public account or her personal one? You said there were multiple accounts?" asked Finn.

"Yeah, Finn. This was on her work-focused account - she gives facials and stuff at a doctor's office, I think. Anyway, it's not really a work account, as much as pushing face creams she uses and highlighting her sequined lifestyle. Pretty amateurish."

"But it's public?"

"Definitely - because I got on it to post and I know for sure that I'm not on her friends list," I said with a smirk.

"Okay, so maybe the arsonist saw your post."

"That's scary," added Megan. "I never think about who's reading my posts and how public they are."

"Me neither," I agreed, shaking my head.

"And if the arsonist saw your post and the first fire was to cover a killing related to blackmail over the money laundering, then the subsequent fires could be to burn any further proof of the money laundering activity the arsonist thought you may possess."

"And the murder linked to the money laundering," Megan added.

"But all I said was that I could prove adultery."

"No, didn't you also say she was a stripper?" Megan asked.

"Yeah, I think so."

"Well, if you can prove she was a stripper, then you have records about the strip club. Divorce is always about money, so everybody assumes there are lots of financial records, too. Maybe that combination made someone nervous," said Finn.

"Nervous enough to come to Connecticut and burn her storage locker and her car?" asked Megan.

"Yep," said Finn. "Because those records could tie this person to money laundering, arson, and murder. You just didn't know what you had."

"So now what?" I asked.

"Now we prove it," said Finn. "I'm just not sure how, and we still don't know who. There's pressure to solve this from Croft's legal team at Yale and my Chief. Croft is running out of time, and from what we have so far, I'm not at all sure he's guilty."

"Shouldn't we take what we have to his lawyers?" asked Megan.

"Not yet," I replied. "We only have circumstantial evidence and a theory of the original crime, and neither is enough to get a new trial for Croft. Not even enough to get an emergency stay on the execution. We need something concrete. We need proof. Plus, I'm about to point a finger at my ex. I know it sounds crazy, but I'm nervous to do that without more. I'm about to do something that will have a huge impact on my kids' lives, and I want to be sure before I do that."

"I hear you," said Finn. "But it's not going to be up to you, Maggie. Once I have probable cause, I have to move on this."

"I know. I just hope it's enough. If we go forward with this and accuse Ted and it doesn't stick, I'm afraid I'll lose my kids. They'll never forgive me. Plus, my family calls Ted 'Teflon' because nothing ever sticks to him, so this has got to be solid."

We each sat quietly, finishing our lunches, and then sat back.

"I have an idea," said Megan. "Although I know I'm not the professional here."

"Let's hear it," said Finn.

"Well, we're focused on the one strip club we know about, the Brass Ass, and her ex's spending there. But didn't your NYPD detective friend say Ted would expand his operation, and that's how he would make more money? Maggie, since the club burned down in 2011, hasn't Ted maintained his lifestyle?"

"Yeah, definitely. If anything, his spending has gone way up. Designer everything and fancy apartments, cars, and vacations, according to my kids."

"Well, then I assume he found another club or clubs to work with and pulled the same scam. He could have brought his clients from the Brass Ass along with him. We just need to find the new clubs."

I looked at Finn as a smile crept across his face.

"Don't underestimate the new girl," Finn said. "I should have enough suspicious activity of money laundering that I can make a request to the banks Ted uses under the PATRIOT Act to look for more money laundering. I hope the records they send will show the new partner club names."

"But will Ted know? We don't want to tip him off," I commented, worried.

"Nope, that's the beauty of the PATRIOT Act. It was passed after 9/11 to expose terrorist financing. It requires banks to help law enforcement trace money when there is suspected money laundering. We used it in New York all the time. It actually has a criminal penalty for tipping off the target, so Ted will never know."

"Wow. Kind of 'big brother' to me," commented Megan. "But I guess if it catches Ted, I approve," she shrugged.

I laughed and hugged Megan and signaled to the waitress for our bill. "And it would be proof of money laundering and a motive for all the arsons," I added.

"Well, be patient. They have 30 days to respond to my request, and it all has to go through the proper channels. I can make a broad request - all banks or at least the big ones - so we'll see what we get. Fingers crossed."

"At least we have a plan," said Megan.

"Indeed, we do," said Finn. "And a solid one at that. I'll brief my chief when I get back to the office and get the paperwork started."

"One other idea," I added. "About the fire in my car."

"Yeah?" asked Finn, leaning in.

"Well, I'm assuming it was spontaneous. You said the arson report said it was like a Molotov cocktail, right?"

"Yeah, that's right. They found the broken bottle pieces. But this time, no fingerprints," said Finn.

"If it was spontaneous, that means the arsonist was watching my house, and then when they saw us load the car with the file boxes, they devised the plan to burn it. It also means they likely did not come to my house prepared."

"So?" asked Megan.

"So, where did they get the bottle of alcohol? Package stores generally have cameras, so maybe we'll get lucky and see someone buying the liquor they used."

"Great idea. I'll get on it as soon as I get back to the station. I'll call you later, Maggie, with an update on both lines of inquiry."

With that, he grabbed the check, refused to split it, and went to the cashier to pay.

"Sounds like now we have to be patient," concluded Megan.

"Yep. Not really a virtue of mine, but I'll try," I shrugged with a grin and hugged her again.

❖

Chapter 20 – A Dark Figure

Finn's update the following afternoon was hopeful. He and an officer had canvased local liquor stores for video footage from the evening and night of the car fire. They had gathered four videos, and he wanted me to come into the station to review them and see if I recognized anybody. He also had gotten the bank requests out for any accounts linked to Ted. I had barely hung up the phone before I shoved my feet into my trusty L.L. Bean boots, pulled on my coat, patted Pumpkin goodbye, and was out the door.

Finn had set up the small conference room with a computer that would play the DVD recordings. He and Officer DeCarlo were waiting when I arrived, and they ushered me in, taking my coat. I followed them into the small room and took a seat.

"So, you just want me to go through these and see if I recognize anyone?" I asked.

"Yep, that's about it. I will be watching with you to try and identify the purchaser, and then you can see if it's someone you might know," said Finn. "DeCarlo, can you bring us some water? I think this is gonna take a while."

"No problem," Officer DeCarlo said, leaving the room and pulling the door behind himself.

By the time he returned with a pitcher and two plastic cups, the first video was rolling. Each video began at 5 pm, and then Finn fast-forwarded between customers until we got to the time of the fire. We saw a lot of beer purchases punctuated by wine but agreed we were looking for cheap, hard alcohol. There were fewer purchases in that category, and the video quality wasn't great, so we were going by the shape and color of the bottle as we reviewed the footage.

On the third DVD, we saw a person dressed in black with a flapped hunting hat, bulky puffer jacket, and dark winter boots picking up a cheap bottle of vodka and bringing it to the counter. Leaving their gloves on, they paid in cash. They turned and left the store, never raising their head to the camera for a clear view of their face below the hat visor.

"That's got to be the guy, don't you think?" I said, hitting pause.

"Well, it's certainly possible that we just saw the arsonist buying what they used to start the fire in your car. But there's no way to know who it was from this video. Plus, they left their gloves on, which explains the lack of fingerprints this time. Anything about the person look familiar?"

"I wish I could say yes. But, no."

Finn rewound the video, and we watched it again.

"What about their height, weight, gait, anything?" he prodded.

"Well, that person looks like they're shorter than six feet, given their frame in the doorway. If it's an arsonist for hire, I wouldn't know them, but maybe I would recognize them if they've been hanging around. It's hard to tell, with that coat, the shape of the person. As to the gait, the person doesn't walk enough for me to tell if I recognize them from anywhere. The winter clothes completely obscure them but aren't suspicious like they would be in the summer. Sorry, I thought this would help, but it's just another mystery."

"Not at all. It was a great idea, and we were able to pinpoint where he bought the accelerant. I'll interview the store clerk to see if they remember anything about the buyer."

"Okay. This is kind of a letdown; I was hoping for a breakthrough," I said with a shrug.

"That's the nature of police work, Maggie. You know that. It's the slow, plodding work that gets the details that will make our case, and this is a good lead. I'll run it down tomorrow."

"I know, I know," I pulled on my coat, and Finn walked me out to my car.

"I'll be over when I'm done here," said Finn as I got into my rental.

"Thanks," I said. "Pasta tonight? It feels like a comfort food night to me."

"Sounds great; I'll grab a bottle of red on my way over. See you in about an hour."

When I got home, I FaceTimed MJ to update her on our progress and lack thereof. She hadn't found anything new in all the documentation but had created a spreadsheet of the accounts identified and another trying to document the movement of funds. She promised to send both over later that night. I also told her of the promise I had elicited from Croft's Yale defense clinic lawyers that morning to pay her their standard investigator rate for her time. I knew it wasn't her normal rate, but at least she wasn't working for free anymore. I gave her their contact details, and we signed off.

I called Megan as I started the sauce for dinner and filled her in on the videos and the dark figure we had seen buying the liquor. We chatted more about her day and the ups and downs of the coffee shop business and even brainstormed other income ideas for Grounded until my doorbell rang.

I opened the door to Finn with Pumpkin at my heels. They followed me into the kitchen, where Finn poured us each a glass of chianti. I got water boiling and then dropped in the pasta.

"To a productive day," said Finn, raising his glass.

"Slàinte," I said in my best Gaelic accent, and we each took a sip. The full-bodied red warmed me on its way down. I stirred the noodles and asked, "But was it really? Felt like a lot of dead ends."

"For sure," nodded Finn. "This is police work. It's not like the movies, but you know that from your days in the D.A.'s office. Our work is usually painstaking and can be slow, but that's how we build a case. Brick by brick. Today, it felt like the foundation of our case had been poured. And we are starting to find the bricks we will need to build."

"I wish I was as optimistic as you are."

"Just try and be patient. We're doing all the right things. It'll all start to come together soon. I'm sure of it."

I served each of us a mound of pasta Bolognese, grated Parmesan across each pile, and we sat at the kitchen table. I was twirling my pasta onto my fork when Finn leaned forward to catch my eye, "Penny, for your thoughts?"

I smiled while taking a huge mouthful of pasta and chewed, holding up a finger to ask for time.

"You could tell how far away I was, couldn't you? It's hard to explain. I put my divorce and all the pain of that time behind me. I really did. But this is opening up all sorts of old wounds I thought had healed. Re-reading my divorce paperwork is harder than I thought it would be. Believe it or not, even after all I know about Ted, it's still hard to wrap my head around who he really is. I know that sounds daft."

Finn started to interrupt.

"Let me get this out, okay? I want to explain, but I also want to understand for myself, and maybe this will help me, too. I've not told anyone a lot about this before. It's why it was so hard to come to you in the first place, I think. It's embarrassing that I was ever with this guy. He was supposed to be the great love of my life." I took a deep, shaking breath and then exhaled slowly.

"That last Christmas we were together, I gave him an album of our love letters from over the years. I stupidly still thought we were a great love story. So, when everything came out like it did, it was impossible to absorb. I didn't just discover that my husband cheated. The psychologists said he was a sociopath and a sex addict. They said the only option was divorce. I knew it was the right thing, but I don't think I have ever really processed what those labels meant, even though I've helped my kids process it for all these years."

I paused, letting my thoughts go back to that day in the therapist's office with Teddy. He didn't react when she declared him a sociopath. I remember watching him, waiting for him to object in outrage, to defend himself. Instead, he sat so still I wondered if he was frozen.

Then he calmly got up and said, "I guess there's nothing left to discuss," and left.

I pitched forward in the therapist's chair as if he had punched me in the stomach. He had become a stranger in an instant, and that terrified me.

I roused myself from the dark memory, continuing to Finn, "When I spent any time thinking about the implications of his diagnosis on my life, it was too much. We were married for thirteen years but were together about nineteen. The reality was I married a guy who was incapable of love. The red flags I should have seen I thought were part of a wonderful parade, not a warning as they should have been.

"Throughout our marriage, Ted never argued. Whenever I got upset with him, Ted dismissed my feelings, saying that I was uptight and overreacted until, by the end, I even started to believe it. Later, once I understood his personality disorder, I saw the gaslighting for what it was. He never argued because to argue, you must first care. That knowledge hurt as much as it explained."

Finn reached across the small table and held my hand.

"But, at the time, I obviously didn't know any of this. So, I pushed all of his behavior aside and got on with the reality of raising three kids. He traveled every week for his consulting work, so I was a single mom for five out of seven days. Once we separated and then divorced, I was co-parenting with someone who was a nightmare. He no longer hid who he really was and was cruel and manipulative."

'I'm so sorry, Maggie. I can't imagine. But how could someone manipulate you? You are so strong and sure of yourself."

'It turns out it's not that hard when you have kids. Once, I was on a date on a lovely Sunday afternoon. I was supposed to pick up the kids at five, but Ted called me at two. He said if I didn't come that moment to get them, he wouldn't turn them over to me at all. I left my date immediately to pick them up. When I arrived, Carter was crying. When I asked what was wrong, he said that their dad had heard about my date from them and was teaching them a lesson."

"What possible lesson?" asked Finn, incredulous.

"That he could always make me do anything he wanted because of them."

"Good God," murmured Finn.

"He was cruel, especially to Ruby. He seemed to target her. On her seventh birthday, he took her to a flower shop and told her to pick the most beautiful arrangement she saw. She was thrilled as she had never gotten flowers before. After she picked a bouquet, he said, 'These are for Amber. Here's twenty bucks; now, pick something for yourself. I'll wait outside.'" I paused as tears spilled down my cheeks. "Every time I think of that beautiful, hopeful little girl, my heart breaks."

"That's horrific," said Finn.

I added, "Once, he left Ruby alone in a park and hid with the other two kids behind a tree as he watched her panic, believing she had been abandoned. His behavior was horrific, and there was nothing I could do to protect them."

"I just can't imagine any father doing that. Couldn't you stop visitation?" asked Finn.

"When they came home to me after these visits and relayed what had happened, I tried to fight for them and limit his visitation or at least have it supervised. My lawyer said it wasn't enough. Ted always walked the line and pulled back just before he went too far."

I paused, taking a deep, shaking breath, before I continued, "Carter, as the oldest, was the first to reach thirteen years old. In Florida, the courts let the kids have a say in visitation at that point. So, I sat him down and offered that he didn't have to go to his dad's anymore." I paused again.

"How did he react?" prodded Finn.

"He said he couldn't leave his sisters alone there. He said he had to keep going until Meryl was thirteen and could stop too." My lips quivered as I said the words and I wept, remembering my son's steeled face as he explained his reasoning to me.

Finn reached up and stroked my cheek, brushing the tears away, as I continued, "And now this. The rational part of me knows he is capable of all of this, but another part of me still says this is unbelievable. I know that sounds naive. I'm a criminologist, for Christ's sake. I know one in twenty people is a sociopath. But when it's this personal, it becomes too much to process and, honestly, really scary."

"I'm here for you now, Maggie; you're not alone anymore."

"Thank you, Finn. That means more to me than you could know." I paused, collecting myself, and sipped my wine. Then added, "You hear people say 'I know everything about my husband' or 'my husband would never do that,' and I know I even said those kinds of things at one time. Now I know it's naive. My husband was a calculated, cold-blooded sociopath. Even as I say it, I disassociate from that reality and what it still means for me and my kids. To even contemplate that he is back in my life and the one potentially starting these fires is terrifying. And I can't even think about Tiffany Schmidt and what happened to her. It will devastate my kids if he did any of this, but I can't imagine the impact if he is also a killer."

I paused, taking a deep breath before I continued.

"They had to find a way to rationalize visits with him weekly and persevere in their love of him, despite his abhorrent behavior, for the last fifteen years. That's why this is such a big deal to me and why I had to be pretty sure of my facts before I came to you. He's put them through so much already. I couldn't bear to do anything to cause them more pain."

I paused again and took a jagged breath, trying to calm the thoughts that were racing through my mind.

I shrugged and tried to smile, "I know this is a huge turn-off in a ton of ways. But you asked, and I want to be honest about the baggage I'm carrying - for me and my children. I want you to know what you're getting into."

I swallowed hard and then quickly took a gulp of wine, trying to avoid any eye contact.

Finn got up and walked around to me, pulling me up into his arms without saying a word. He hugged me, and I could feel his heartbeat and his breath move in and out. We didn't move for a long time, and I realized tears were sliding down my face and onto his shirt. I started to pull away, but he pulled me back into an embrace. And I wept against him in relief, in fear, and in dread of the Pandora's box we were opening.

❖

Chapter 21 – The Little Things

I woke the next morning to the sun streaming in my windows but feeling hungover from the emotion of the previous night. Finn was gone but had left a note on the kitchen table that he'd see me later. I drank coffee while sitting on the floor with Pumpkin.

"What do you think, old girl? Have I finally gone round the bend? Finn must think so. Do you?"

I massaged her velvety ears between my fingers and looked into her deep, brown eyes.

"You won't leave me, will you? We'll be crazy old ladies together."

Pumpkin harrumphed, puffing her cheeks out and exhaling as though to say, "Speak for yourself."

"Okay, okay, just me then," I said, rubbing her head and pulling myself to my feet.

"I gotta get going, or I'll be late for class."

***

I stood, leaning against the lectern and looking out at my students, "Okay, let's pick up where we left off. I asked you to come back with a criminal profile. Who are we dealing with in these pattern arsons?"

"And we were gonna get our hands on the divorce paperwork too, right?" prodded Liam.

"I put our request to the police, and they said they would consider it. They are working the financials themselves with the help of the banks involved. In the meantime, we can work on the criminal profile. Who are we dealing with?"

"It's a cover-up," suggested Josie. "The latest fires were to cover for the first one, but even the first one was to cover a murder. You said Tiffany died from a blow to the head, right? So, all of them are to cover something up."

"If that's the case, then you are positing that the motive is really about the killing of Tiffany Schmidt. The rest of it is about self-preservation?" I asked. "Do we know why she was killed? Was it a personal motive, or could it have been driven by the finances we have been discussing?"

The class agreed that without more on the divorce financials, we couldn't intuit more about the motive for the murder.

I pivoted, asking, "What kind of killer stays engaged this long? Again, I ask you, who are we dealing with?"

"Someone who's patient, a planner," offered Liam. "Also, close enough to the players in the original crime to stay abreast of developments over ten years. There had to have been a trigger for the more recent fires, and that likely ties in with the divorce and the ex-husband. He's the only link, right?"

"Yeah, that's right, Liam," agreed Josie. "The ex-wife's stuff is burned because something she has sheds light on the original crime. She must have triggered the recent fires somehow."

"Let's not blame the ex-wife," said Liam. "She probably doesn't even know what she has."

I smiled at Liam's defense of the ex-wife. "Okay, so Tiffany's killer was not a stranger. This was someone who knew her and the other players in the frame and stayed in touch with them for over a decade. That contact could have been either because the killer was part of their world naturally, or because they made sure they were to continue the cover-up of their original crime. Either way, it's nearly worked because Croft is nearing execution. I think a date will be set in the next couple of months," I summarized for the class. "So how do we identify the perpetrator, or perp as the police would say, based on our criminal profile?"

The students spent the rest of our time throwing out ideas, which, in the end, we all agreed, would not work. As they filed out of the classroom, Liam stopped at my desk, holding Josie back with him.

"I don't want to overstep, Professor Glass," he started. "But I googled the crimes."

Josie looked at him perplexed, unsure of where he was going.

"And you found out I'm the ex-wife," I admitted.

"What?" said Josie, looking between Liam and me.

"It's not a state secret, and it's in the public record. It was bound to come out," I said.

"Are you okay?" asked Josie, touching my arm.

"I'm fine, or I will be, once all this is done and dusted."

"How can we help?" asked Liam.

"Yeah, what can we do?" added Josie.

"You're already doing it by helping me figure out who is behind al this."

As they both nodded, I continued, "The police are running down lead and shrinking the frame, but this is so personal to me that I want to help them however I can."

"Of course," said Josie.

"In the meantime, please keep my involvement to yourselves. I someone asks you directly, don't lie, but just don't offer it up if you don't mind. It's all rather Jerry Springer if you know what I mean," said with a smile, trying to lighten the mood.

"Who's Jerry Springer?" asked Josie, tilting her head.

I laughed out loud, "A sleazy talk show host from when I was you age. His guests were always involved in seedy sex scandals. mentioned him because this is all rather embarrassing, and I'm stil new to the university. I'd rather not be dragged back into my ex husband's sordid life if I can help it."

"Got it," said Liam, and Josie nodded in agreement, saying. "We won't out you, Professor Glass."

"Thanks, guys," I said as I walked them out of the classroom.

***

Finn came over after work with takeout Chinese. I emptied the containers onto plates and set out both chopsticks and forks, just ir case. I opened a beer for each of us, and we sat at the kitchen table.

"So? I'm dying. Any progress?" I prodded.

"I spoke to the clerk at the liquor store. They don't remember the person specifically. Nothing there."

"I figured that would be the case, but I had hope. Man or woman? Anything?" I asked.

"Nope, no memory. I got the impression the clerk spends a lot of time smoking pot. Maybe even while at work. His house was littered with paraphernalia, and Grateful Dead posters covered his walls."

"Rats."

"I also ran background checks on your ex and his wife. There's a story there," he said, raising his eyebrows.

"Yeah, I know a lot of it from the private investigator in my divorce."

"Ted has a history of running out on his debts. There are hundreds of thousands in IRS and credit card liens and even garnishments when the creditors can get them. Hell, even the Ft. Lauderdale Yacht Club went after him. But that all dates back to around the time of your divorce. More recently, he has had huge credit card bills again but seemingly keeps up with them. He doesn't pay them off, but he floats them month to month with just enough paid to keep the creditors at bay. His credit is non-existent, which may explain why I can't find any property or vehicles that are owned by him. Seems everything is rented or leased. He also has an ongoing record of traffic violations - mostly speeding. It's so bad that he's faced license suspension in Florida, Kentucky, Texas, and Ohio. Again, he's managed to avoid that in each case, but just barely."

"Yep, all that was discovered at trial, but I didn't know it was ongoing. Although I have heard from my kids that he still struggles with debt, it worries them."

"Amber has less of a paper trail. Same huge credit card bills which she floats along, and she doesn't own anything."

"Not surprising, I guess. She was just a stripper until she met Ted."

"There are some interesting entries on their rap sheets, though," he paused. "This is a little delicate."

"I think I know some of it. The investigator for my divorce lawyer got copies of summonses in Cleveland for indecent exposure in a park for both of them. He spoke to the arresting officer, and apparently, they were having sex on a park bench," I rolled my eyes. "Classy, I know. And Ted was convicted of criminal contempt during my divorce trial for lying to the judge about emptying our retirement funds."

"I'd say you're kidding, but I know you're not. But I didn't see the contempt on his rap sheet. I'm not sure why that conviction doesn't show up."

"I know why, I think. He was convicted of contempt in Florida family court, and they never followed through to get it on his record. Not surprising, Teddy always slithers out of everything. Anything on Amber?"

"Before her marriage to your ex, she was picked up on check kiting, shoplifting, and solicitation - all were pled out to community service or just dismissed. She's a sad story. Once she married Ted though, it's clean. Pretty obvious that she went from having nothing to having it all."

"Yeah, when Ted met her, she was living week to week in a motel across the street from the club where she stripped. I don't know much about her except that she didn't graduate high school. Left home early and was on her own until she met my ex. Pretty common tale, unfortunately. Women don't dream of growing up to be strippers. They're all pretty desperate for one reason or another."

"Yeah, pretty sad," added Finn. "But not sure it justifies the havoc she has wrought on your life."

"I agree," I said. "But I see her as pathetic. She was like a trapped animal who would do anything to survive. I almost can't blame her." I grimaced, adding, "Almost." And then changed the subject.

"My class discussed all of the facts and hypothesized that the Connecticut fires have been to cover up the original crime in Texas. There was some debate about what crime they were covering up, but the resulting behavior was the same - arson. What we couldn't agree on was how to prove it."

"Yeah, I think our best hope is the bank records," replied Finn.

"Anything we can do in the meantime?" I asked, hopefully.

"Not that you can do, but I am still running down the information with the banks and reading the paperwork."

"Thanks, Finn. I'm just so anxious about all of this. One thought - Ted and Amber live in Florida. Maybe the clubs he works with now are down there rather than Texas?"

"Good point. That might help us focus any results we get from the banks. Megan had suggested looking for club names, too. Narrowing the clubs to Florida to look for new partners should help speed things up, I hope. I know you want this all to move faster, but we need to take our time and follow procedure to ensure we get the right outcome. If Croft has been wrongfully convicted and put on death row, the last thing I want to do is make a mistake and put another innocent person in his place."

"I know, I know. But can we be careful and still follow the process quickly?" I asked with a smile.

Finn burst out laughing, and I couldn't help but laugh too. We cleaned up the remaining Chinese food and spent the rest of the evening not talking about the case.

❖

Chapter 22 – A Game

The weekend was brisk and overcast, with a February sky as we scoured the car lots in New Haven for my new car. I hoped for something fun and sporty, reflecting the new life I wanted to build for myself in Bell Harbor. Finn countered that it needed to perform well in snowy conditions. After much debate, I opted for a yellow Mini Cooper, much to Finn's amusement. I drove the sunshine-colored car off the lot, thrilled with my new purchase, and christened her Tulip during the ride home.

Despite my new wheels, the following week dragged on. I tried my best to be mentally present as I taught and held office hours daily, but my mind was elsewhere. I was constantly checking my phone for an update from Finn.

On Friday, I couldn't take it anymore and gave in when my class asked me to brainstorm the case again. After going round and round and getting nowhere, Josie spoke up.

"I think we should try to catch the ex-husband in a sting to find out what he knows and prove one way or the other if he is involved. Use his psychology against him."

"How so?" I asked, interested in where she was going.

"Well, the ex-husband is a sociopath. That means a lot more than just that he's unable to have emotions. He assumes everyone is like him and is working an angle, lying, and cheating. It also means he doesn't fear consequences and is always playing a game, or at least trying to play. Maybe we can figure out some way to turn the tables on him using his own psychology."

"We're talking about murder and arson, Josie. Getting involved like that would be dangerous. All we can do is help direct the police in their lines of inquiry," I said, realizing I couldn't involve my class any further.

"That's no fun," said Liam. "I want to do something."

"We are doing something," I replied. "We're developing real theories of the crimes to help guide the police and develop new leads. This is what criminologists do and it really does help the authorities. Just think of the TV show *Criminal Minds*. They develop theories of the crimes that help the police identify both lines of inquiry and even descriptions of persons of interest. That's what we can do here. We can make a real impact."

"Yeah, that's pretty cool," conceded Liam. "Have we done that?"

"Well, we've helped focus them on the original crime. That's where a mistake is more likely, where the motive for the later crimes is hidden. We have to hope that's enough," I added as the bell rang.

The class filed out, and I remained in place, wondering if that really was enough this time and whether or not Josie and Liam were right about needing to do more.

*****

Early the following week, Finn finally texted that he had started to hear back from the banks. In all, four banks had responded positively about having accounts in Ted or Amber's name. But they were all vague in their responses and needed to be spoken to in order to pry loose more details. Finn spoke to each of them by the end of the week, and on Saturday morning, I made pancakes and invited Finn and Megan over to go through the results.

Finn spread out his notes, leaving room for his plate, a pool of syrup with an island of pancakes. Megan and I each served ourselves, and I topped up everyone's coffee so we could sit and listen.

"Well, it's like we thought, he's laundering money, and I think the banks agree with us."

"Why do you think that?" I asked.

"They all mentioned SARs, Suspicious Activity Reports. You have to file those reports with FinCEN, the Financial Crimes Enforcement Network, if you have reasonable cause to believe you've identified money laundering or terrorist financing. The fact that they each have made SAR filings means they believe or at least have reasonable cause to believe there is money laundering in his accounts."

I started to jump in, "But what-"

"Let me keep going," continued Finn. "They each also asked me what other banks had responded positively, and now they are all talking. The likely next step is the closure of his bank accounts. However, the government could ask them to delay that action if it compromises any ongoing criminal investigation."

"Oh, crap. Then he'll know we're on to him," I said, shaking my head.

"Not necessarily," said Finn. "After all, the banks already had him on their radar. Plus, it's a crime to tip off a FinCEN target, which should buy us some time."

He used his fingers to add air parentheses to the words tip-off.

We spent the next hour reviewing the details he had gotten from each bank, account numbers, co-owners, and large money movements. The only pattern we saw was significant money movement in and then frequent smaller movements out to accounts in Amber's name only. Then, movement out of Amber's account of the total amount, often to multiple accounts in Ted's name. We also saw other accounts at offshore banks that weren't subject to the PATRIOT Act, so we couldn't find out more about those. However, we could see large amounts moving into them and nothing returning, so they seemed to be a final destination. Or at least as far as our paper trail could follow.

After we had gone through it all, I asked, "Now what? We see the motive for a cover-up, but we don't have anything to tie him to the arsons. What do we do?"

Finn responded, "We may still hear from more banks, especially after they speak to one another."

"Yeah, but what would that add?" asked Megan

"Not much," I chimed in. "We need something substantive. We need an admission."

"How do we get that?" Megan asked.

"I get it," I replied.

"No way," said Finn, standing up and starting to pace in front of us.

I jumped up to meet him and held his shoulders to stop the pacing, "You know I'm right; there's no other way."

"There has to be. If we're right, Ted and Amber either committed or are linked to a murder and three arsons – it's too dangerous."

"I agree with Finn," said Megan. "It seems way too risky. Isn't there anything else we can do?"

"I'm open to alternatives," I said. "But Steve Croft is on death row. If he dies, I'll never forgive myself for not doing everything in my power to save him."

Neither Finn nor Megan disagreed with that statement, and Finn began to pace again as I sat back down. We all knew I was right; we had nothing concrete linking Ted to the crimes, and Croft was running out of time.

Finally, Megan said, "Let's come up with a plan that we can all be comfortable with - that doesn't expose you too much. If you stay safe, then I'm all in. I agree that we have to do something because of Croft. Plus, whoever is doing this has targeted you now twice. I don't want to give them a third try."

We spent the rest of the morning and into the afternoon debating the best path forward but resolving nothing.

"Let's take a break," said Finn, while squeezing the bridge of his nose. "We need to clear our heads."

"Good idea," chimed in Megan. "I'll go check in at the store. Maybe if we step back, the solution will present itself."

"Maybe," I said half-heartedly.

After they both left, I sank into the couch with Pumpkin. I was so full of emotions I couldn't name them all. I was scared that Ted was guilty and what that meant for my kids. I was anxious that he wasn't, and I was putting something in motion that would ensnare him needlessly and hurt my kids. It seemed anything I did would end badly for the people I loved the most in this world. But how could I ignore all I knew? If I didn't act, an innocent man could die. If Ted was guilty, he would get away with murder. What did that make me? I got up and changed into my running gear. To Pumpkin's chagrin, I didn't take her with me. I ran and ran, past our usual turning point, and then sprinted until I couldn't breathe. I halved at the waist, hands on my knees, gasping for cold winter air to clear the jumble of thoughts in my head. Fifteen years ago, I had left Ted to be a good example to my kids, despite how painful it was.

I knew what I had to do now.

I jogged home, and by the time I opened the front door, a plan had started to form. To confront Ted, I had to use all I had learned about him and my experience - I had to meet a sociopath in the only way he would understand and appreciate - by playing a game. I showered and texted Megan and Finn to come back for dinner.

They both showed up just as the pizza was arriving. I laid the boxes open on the dining table and passed around napkins, plates, and bottles of beer. My demeanor must have signaled to them a change because they were both silent as we began to eat.

After we each had our first bite, I said, "We need to play a game with him. It's all he'll understand. We need him to engage and play in order to get him to let his guard down."

"But won't his guard be up if he's playing a game?" asked Megan. "Won't he know you're up to something?"

"Not if we do this right," I said, winding the cheese around the end of a slice as I pulled it from the pie. "Ted's so cocky he always assumes he's the smartest in the room. He'll think he's in control, and we'll let him."

"Let's hear the plan then," replied Finn, all business.

"Well, child support ends next year. The exact date was determined by his payments toward the total number owed. Both of us agreed on the total, but the end date is still under debate."

"How can that be if the total is agreed?" asked Megan.

"Because there is a typo in the agreement placing the end date three months shy of when the total will actually be paid. It is a small typo, but Ted is clinging to it despite my asking him to amend it to match the agreed total. It is enough to make a difference in Meryl's tuition payments for her final year of school, so I have continued to ask him about it. He, as usual, has dragged the back and forth out, and made it clear that he won't pay past the current date in the agreement."

"So how does this help us?" prodded Megan.

"Well, it's an opening into his finances," I answered.

"You'd threaten to take him to court over the typo correction?" asked Finn.

"No, not exactly. That wouldn't help us. I thought I could threaten to take him back to court over the typo with the twist that I would also contest his income levels retroactively - saying he perjured himself when he provided his financials in the divorce. That would trigger a full financial review by the court."

"Isn't there a statute of limitations or something?" asked Megan. "I thought you guys were divorced like fifteen years ago?"

"There's no statute of limitations for this stuff, but a judge probably wouldn't allow me to go back that far. It's not fair or reasonable. However, he kept me in court for eight years past the end of our divorce fighting the child support, and now this support agreement needs to be corrected, and we have proof he misrepresented his finances, so that could potentially open the whole thing up."

"I still don't get how this helps us," said Finn. "Seems to me all you'd be doing is poking a bear."

"This is where the game starts," I said. "Ted never sees other people playing him because he thinks he's so smart. So, if I threaten him with the financial review to get the current agreement updated, he won't question it. But I won't stop there. I'll tell him I know about the money laundering and that the proof I have didn't burn in the fire. I'll tell him I'll go to the police unless he not only updates the agreement but adds to it."

"Would he believe you'd do that?" asked Megan, tilting her head in a puzzled expression.

"Yeah," added Finn. "That doesn't sound like you."

"That's the thing about sociopaths, though; they believe anyone is capable of anything because they are. It will never occur to him that something else is going on. He'll believe the surface motive of greed and never suspect I'm trying to get him to talk about money laundering. And I'll get him on tape."

"And how do you do this safely?" asked Finn with a scowl.

"I'll tell him that the proof will go to the authorities if anything happens to me."

"They say that in the movies all the time," said Megan. "And it never works. Someone always ends up dead. We need a better way to protect you."

We all sat in silence, pondering a better plan until Megan continued, "The reason they end up dead is because the target always asks the blackmailer if they have told anyone else, and they say 'no.' First of all, why would a blackmailer ever admit they haven't told anyone else when asked? Anyway, once they admit that no one else knows, the blackmailer gets killed, and the killer rushes to find the evidence before it is released. We obviously don't want that outcome. So, what if Maggie starts out by saying the police already have the evidence, which is true, but they haven't connected the dots? She's given the rest of the proof to two other people who both will provide it to the police should anything happen to her?"

"It needs to be stronger than that. I think she could also let him know that she has documented what she is doing so that if anything happens to her, the police will know it was him," added Finn.

"One other thing worries me," I said. "Blackmailers get killed because of the fear that the payments will never stop - even if they say it's a one-time thing. How do I counter that? If he knows the payments will end, then I am safer. Remember, he will assume I will act as he would and that I am not trustworthy."

"Ooh, good point," said Megan. "How can we assure him this is a one-time deal?"

With that, we all fell silent again.

After several minutes, I said, "My kids."

"What do you mean?" asked Finn.

"The only thing he will believe is if it has to do with protecting my kids. He knows I would do anything for them. So somehow, we need to tie the one-time payment to them."

"How?" asked Megan.

"He doesn't trust anyone, but he knows I'd do anything for my kids. He trusts my motive when it comes to them. He's even told them that he knew he would always be able to manipulate me because of my love for them."

"He told them that? That's sick," interrupted Megan.

"Separate conversation, but the point is that it's a motive he'll believe. So, we need to use it somehow to protect me."

"What if we go back to the truth?" asked Megan. "All along, you've told me you wanted to be sure before you said anything to the police about Ted because it could hurt your children. Would he believe you'd keep his secret to protect them?"

"I think he would," I replied. "But I don't think he would be comfortable letting that be enough. He wouldn't like that the power dynamics of our relationship had changed. He wouldn't like that I had something on him. We need to get him comfortable again and convince him that he is still in control to keep me safe."

"So maybe the extra payment you request is for your kids. Graduate school or something. And maybe it's big enough that he has to move money in from those off-shore accounts," suggested Megan.

You're onto something," added Finn. "If we can get him to move money from those foreign bank accounts, we wouldn't need him to admit everything. It would get us the information we can't reach through all of our PATRIOT Act requests. But we still need a reason why he'd believe it's a one-off demand and you won't come back for more."

"We could tie it to the current agreement that ends in a year. I could say everything needs to be paid as part of the current agreement we're amending. His additional payment will be added to the contract, and I could also sign a non-disclosure agreement, which would protect him. Plus, this makes him look like a hero to our kids, and the non-disclosure agreement would keep me from telling them I contracted for it. It's a win-win for him. What do you think?" I asked while beginning to wring my hands.

"One question," asked Megan. "Can you have an NDA to cover up a crime like money laundering?"

"It's okay. It's not to cover a crime, just to keep me from bringing allegations of a crime to the authorities. Think about all the NDAs famous people use to pay off sexual assault victims to keep them quiet. Same thing. We'd say I'd forfeit everything if I went to the police."

"By George, I think she's got it!" shouted Megan, hopping up and dancing around me.

Her reaction caused us all to burst out laughing as the tension in the room had finally been released. We spent the next hour or so laying out scenarios and potential conversations until we had run out of ideas, and Megan headed home.

Finn stayed long enough to kiss me softly on the lips and hug me tightly, saying, "This whole thing could go sideways, you know. I know he's your ex, but he sounds dangerous, and we still have no idea who he's in business with."

"I know," I said. "But I have to do something, and this is a good plan."

"Okay," Finn said with one more soft kiss. "I'll leave you to get a good night's sleep. We need clear heads tomorrow."

I smiled, knowing sleep would be nearly impossible for me tonight, as I shut and locked the door behind him.

❖

Chapter 23 – The Game is Afoot

It started with an email to Ted, with Amber in copy, as always. Ted tended to ignore or just delete my emails and texts without ever reading them, but I trusted Amber would be sure he saw it.

> Ted,
>
> We still need to revise our support agreement to correct the end date. In addition, I have information that causes me to believe I, and the children, have been woefully underpaid by you over the years. We can either handle this in court, where it will all come out publicly, or we can agree on a fair number with an accompanying NDA that I will sign to have this all go away permanently and silently for you. The amount should enable our kids to avoid student debt for graduate school. Plus, the NDA would stop me from telling the kids of our revised arrangement – you'll be the great dad who voluntarily paid for their education. We'll both know it's a lie, but they never will. We should speak in person. If you will be in New York City for work soon, let me know, and we can meet to iron this all out once and for all.
>
> I expect to hear from you shortly,
>
> Maggie

After Finn, Megan, and I all read and re-read the note, and edited it mercilessly, I hit send. With a swoosh, the game was afoot. But it wasn't a game, and I knew it. Tiffany was dead, someone was starting fires ever closer to my home, and Croft's life hung in the balance. I took a deep, shaking breath and gave a long exhale while gripping the edge of my kitchen table.

We then sent an email to Croft's lawyers at the Yale Legal Defense Clinic. We summarized what we had found in Ted's accounts and attached all the documentation.

"Phew," I said, rubbing the back of my neck while I arched my back against the chair. "I'm glad that part's done."

Both Megan and Finn nodded in agreement as they stood next to me, still gazing at the computer screen.

"Okay," said Finn, with a burst of sudden energy. "That was step one. Now we have to get ready for step two."

We spent the next couple of hours planning where the meeting could occur, what Ted needed to do and say to ensnare himself, and how I could possibly solicit those responses without giving the plan away. After not agreeing on much, we were just about to give up for the day when the Yale lawyers responded.

Dear Maggie,

Thank you for your continued interest in Mr. Croft's case and the work you are doing to unearth potentially exculpatory material. As incriminating as these documents seem to be of your ex-husband for money laundering, we do not see enough of a link to the crime of which Mr. Croft has been convicted to petition for a new trial at this time. That being said, we remain vigilant in his defense and appreciate the information you continue to share. As you know, his time is growing short.

With our profound thanks,

The Yale Defense Clinic

Two days later, an email from Ted arrived, agreeing to meet in Central Park by Bethesda Fountain the following Saturday at five in the afternoon. It was smart of him because he could see 360 degrees around the fountain, but I also felt comfortable because it was public. However, at five, it would be twilight. Park lights would be on, but it would be increasingly hard to see. Finn and I discussed it and decided it was good for us, too, because Finn could stay closer to me under the cover of darkness. And so, I agreed to the meeting on Ted's terms.

The week dragged on. I spent my lectures quizzing my students on how to elicit answers from a suspect, and we agreed that leading questions worked but weren't dispositive - you needed to get the person talking, bragging even.

Josie commented, "With sociopaths, it might even be easier. They're dying to tell you how smart they are, how they tricked you, how they won."

Her point hit home, and I realized I needed to let Ted brag about how he had deceived me for all these years. I needed to let him believe he had won, once and for all.

I remembered the song from the *Mamma Mia* movie, sung by Meryl

Streep, "The Winner Takes It All," and thought how appropriate it was to my life at the moment. Was this really a game between Ted and I and if so, what were the stakes?

I muffled the lyrics blaring in my head and asked the class, "So how do you ask the questions? How do you get a sociopath talking?"

"You tell him you admire him. You ask how he did it. You could even act like you know everything but get it wrong so he can correct you. Let him brag. Let him mock you. Let him show off. But all the time, he's talking. All the time, he's confessing."

Liam high-fived Josie across the aisle when she was done, exclaiming, "Brilliant!"

"That's classic sociopathic behavior," I agreed. "Any other thoughts? Ideas?"

Carrie, a quieter student, raised her hand.

"Yes?" I indicated for her to speak.

"Wouldn't a sociopath know you were playing them? Aren't they experts at this?"

"I suppose they could if you went too far. The detectives would need to be cautious about how they ask their questions and try to get the suspect talking. They would need to play the game better than the sociopath in this case. It sounds hard to do, to your point, Carrie, but remember, sociopaths believe they're smarter than everyone else. They don't think through the consequences of their actions, so the suspect won't assume he's being played. This is all especially true if he believes he has bested this particular questioner before."

The bell rang, and the students filed out. Liam and Josie lingered behind the others.

"Are you really going to confront him?" asked Liam.

"Won't that be dangerous?" added Josie.

"I have to do something. I'm working with the police, so I'll be protected. It'll be fine, and hopefully, all of this will end before someone else gets hurt," I spoke with assurance to calm them, and they left, wishing me luck.

As I packed up my tote, I replayed the class conversation in my mind. The part we hadn't gotten to is what would happen once the sociopath knew he had been bested. And even worse, if he caught me and realized what was going on. A cold chill ran down my back, and I looked around the big, empty room. This plan had to work.

❖

Chapter 24 – The Meet

As I walked into Central Park, dusk was clinging to the trees, and the cold of winter hung in the air as I exhaled. I took a deep breath, breathing in and out to calm my frazzled nerves. My boots crunched in the packed, day-old snow. I was keenly aware of the sounds of the park. A bird flapped above, and a squirrel (or was it a rat?) scurried through the bushes behind me.

A couple walked past me on their way out of the dark and into the lights of the Upper West Side. How bizarre, I thought, they have no idea what I'm about to do. I turned, frightened by the yellow pools cast by the street lights where they blurred into the emerging night, and focused again on the path ahead of me. I picked up my pace. To get to Bethesda Fountain, I had to cross the Strawberry Fields' peace mosaic for John Lennon. A homeless man asleep on a bench by the monument stirred as I passed. I wrapped my arms around myself to stop the shudder that ran down my spine. Was it the cold? Or fear? Was it too late to turn back? I stepped across the peace sign and pressed on.

Peace. Would I finally find it if this plan worked? Since the day I found out about Ted, I'm not sure I've had peace in my life. His behavior forever changed how I saw the world and the people in it. I was always just a little bit afraid. I could remember the girl I was before, who was confident and sure she could do anything. But she seemed so far away now. That is until I moved to Bell Harbor. In my new village home, I had discovered some remnants of her - of the Maggie I used to be. But Ted had found me there, too. Would this meeting finally bring me the peace I needed, or would it only make things worse?

My kids had always said they understood what had happened between their father and me. But Meryl had recently posted for her dad's birthday - #best friend. Ruby had also posted "likes" of Amber's social media posts about her and Ted's romance. Had he so twisted the facts to my kids that they actually believe he is a good person? Someone to be admired? I see him for who he is - cruel, cold, and calculating. No conscious. And Amber? Amber is an opportunist. I have always pitied her for how she was raised and that she resorted to stripping, but that didn't justify what she had done to my family and my life.

As much as the truth of who they were seemed evident to the friends in whom I confided, I never wanted to hurt my kids by telling them everything. I had tried to pick teachable moments. Given the recent public adoration of Ted and Amber from my girls, I see I didn't do enough. But could I have? And should I have? I chose the high road but I was left with them believing the narrative he had spun. When this all comes out - and it seems now that it surely will - will they reject me and defend him? Could I bear it if they did? Will "doing the right thing" be enough to console me for the loss of my kids?

Cut it out, Maggie! I chastised myself. You're freaking yourself out. Your kids will eventually know and understand the truth. Believe in them. I gulped my breath and mentally shook myself back to the reality of the cold winter night and what I was about to do. Finn is here somewhere watching you. You're perfectly safe. I repeated that mantra to myself, hoping I'd believe it. You're perfectly safe. I knew that wasn't true the minute I thought it.

The sidewalk wound through trees and in between bushes whose winter skeletons reached into my path. I gingerly stepped around them and across patches of ice as I hurried to the main road. My eyes darted back and forth, scanning the ground ahead for potholes and more ice. I intermittently broke my scrutiny of my route to look backward over my shoulder and the darkness behind me. When I crested 72nd Street, I saw the steps down to the magnificent Bethesda Fountain, dry now for the winter. It stretched up into the sky, lit by spotlights on its central spire and street lights that circled the open plaza. I saw Ted below, pacing like a tiger in a cage. I stopped and idled in the shadows, gathering my courage. Deep breaths, I told myself. Play the game. I pulled my phone from my coat pocket and began recording before tucking it away again. I pasted a smile on my face and moved into the street light.

I held the railing as I descended towards him to slow and steady my pace. A couple strolled arm-in-arm across Bow Bridge towards me. The still lake behind them reflected the glow of the street lamps along the shore and the ambient light of the city. They passed between Ted and me as I reached the plaza, and then ascended the steps, moving away from us.

Ted looked me up and down and smiled a broad smile that betrayed a coldness in his eyes, saying, "So you showed. I am dying to see what your latest hysteria is all about. Honestly, you're the crazy ex-wife that keeps on giving."

"Not so crazy, as you know," I said as calmly as I could, closing the distance between us. "Or you wouldn't have shown."

Since we had first separated, he had normalized his lack of emotion and reaction by telling the kids that my perfectly normal emotions were overreactions. It was an insidious manipulation of how they saw me and had damaged my relationship with each of them. It was part of the reason I was so fearful of speaking up against him. I knew he would repeat the line that had worked so many times to distance my kids from me - but there was no turning back now.

I took a deep breath to steady my nerves and continued, "I've had to go through some of my old divorce paperwork lately, and I found the strangest thing. A pattern of unusual money movement across your accounts."

He held his smile but still said nothing. His eyes bore into mine.

"I think it shows enough that I can go back to court, with a forensic accountant, of course, to ask for a review of our settlement. You've been holding out on me," I held his gaze.

He rolled his eyes, dismissing me and saying, "Give me a break. You don't have anything. All your documentation is over fifteen years old. If there was anything there, it would have come out at our divorce trial."

"Maybe, if that's what we had been looking for. But we underestimated you. We were just looking for the dissipation of marital assets. This is a whole illegal business you've got going. And a very profitable one at that," I said with a smile and paused, crossing my arms.

"So, turn me in. Go to the police if you've got so much on me. They'll laugh you out of there with your crazy rantings."

"I could go to the police, but I wouldn't say a word. Instead, I'd provide them with this." As I spoke, I reached into my tote and pulled out a file with a few of the account statements we had connected to the money laundering. I waved it in his direction.

"Miss Prosecutor again, I see. Whatever you think you've got, it's nothing. All easily explained. You've never understood business. You're embarrassing yourself now," he crossed his arms across his chest and leaned back against the edge of the fountain, also crossing his ankles, as though fully relaxed. "I showed up to amuse myself. Thanks for the joke. I have friends waiting on me and have to go."

He rose to stand.

"You can go, but you should know that I found the account at Signature Bank. And a friend helped link it to the one you have in St. Maarten. Sure, you don't want to take a peek at these?" I waved the file folder at him again. "I would rather get some of the money you owe me than get you arrested and get nothing. The kids need it. They all have student loans from college and will get more debt for grad school. They shouldn't owe that kind of debt when you have millions in the bank."

"You bitch," he seethed through gritted teeth, rising and crossing to me before I could react. He snatched the folder, pulled off a glove, and leafed through the sheets, scanning the accounts. "This isn't for the kids. You just want the money," he said without looking up.

"I don't, really. You can give it directly to the kids or their schools, whatever you want. We'll update our child support agreement so that this is all over when it expires in a year, and I'll sign an NDA."

"Yeah, like that'll shut your trap," he spit out the words only inches from my face. "I don't think so. You can't do a damn thing to me. If you do, you'll go down too." A slow smile spread across his face. He walked back over to the fountain and resumed his casual stance as his confidence re-emerged, "I told you a long time ago that you'd never be able to tell the truth as well as I could lie. In this case, I don't even have to. Did you check the name on some of those accounts?" He paused for effect. "T. Melody?" He began to laugh, and it echoed in my ears and across the now deserted pavement. "I moved some of it in your name. You stupid bitch, you're in this up to your eyeballs. You can't go to the police, and I'm not paying you another dime."

Amber had impersonated me during our divorce, running up tens of thousands in credit card debt, and clearly, he had used her again. Tara was my grandmother's name and my first name, but it had never felt like me. I always went by my middle name, Margaret. Maggie. Ted had taken advantage of our matching first initials.

I let a beat go by.

"I know," I said slowly and let a small grin cross my face, now matching his.

I paused again, letting the full weight of that statement sink in. "Putting it in my name only works if I don't know about it."

I smiled and mimicked his crossed-arm stance.

After he looked back up at me with his cold, hazel eyes, I added, "The other option is that I just take the money you should have given the kids for school all these years - after all, some of the accounts are still in my name. I know you'd hate that because you wouldn't get credit for giving it to them. Oh, and I'll reimburse myself for the car you burned and the stuff that was in my storage locker."

His jaw clenched hard as he seethed but was silent. That was more terrifying than if he had screamed at me. I knew he was debating his options and calculating his next move. I thought I detected his mask of confidence fall for a milli-second, but I couldn't be sure.

"Oh, yeah, I was sorry to hear about those fires," he finally said with a smirk. "Heard you lost a lot. You're lucky they didn't burn your house with you in it. Or, God forbid, if the kids were visiting. You don't know who you're dealing with, Maggie. Stop bluffing, take your little file, and go back to Bell Harbor."

He threw the file at my feet, and I let it fall. I was too scared to take my eyes off of him.

He winked at me and then turned and walked away. I stood watching him go as he wound up the footpath toward the east. I shuddered, wrapping my arms around myself in a hug. The man I had loved as a young woman was long gone, revealing an empty shell of a human that terrified me. I blew my breath out to calm my nerves. I rolled my shoulders back, trying to release the tension balled at my neck. I picked up the file and stuffed it into my tote. I reached into my pocket, pulled out my phone, and stopped the recording, hoping I had captured enough. I was reeling from the meeting and the venom he had spewed. How had I ever loved that man? How had I not seen him for who he really was from the beginning?

I made my way back up the stairs from the fountain and along the 72nd Street transverse towards the park gate. I played the conversation back in my mind. Did he say enough? Was my bluff enough to throw him off? As I walked up the path, I slipped on the ice and skidded into the bushes whose branches had been so foreboding earlier. As I fell, a shot rang out, and rather than try and catch myself, I let myself fall hard on the frozen ground. I heard quick steps and then the sounds of a struggle. And then another shot. And then a moan. I didn't move. I listened. My heart was hammering in my ears so loudly that I was sure that whoever had fired the gun would hear my heartbeat too and find me. I didn't move. What seemed like an eternity later, I heard footsteps running away. The shoes crunched on gravel, so whoever it was must have run along the bridle path. When the sounds of the steps were gone, I heard the moan again. Who was shot? And then it hit me. Oh my God, Finn. Where was Finn?

I crawled as quietly as I could through the bushes toward the sounds of the moaning. Peering from the overgrowth, I saw Finn lying on the sidewalk on his back. The streetlights cast an eerie yellow tint on his skin. I crawled to him, whispering his name and praying he'd respond. I ran my hands across his chest but didn't find any wound. I checked his head and then lifted it into my lap. With that shift of his torso, he groaned again.

"Oh, thank God, you're alive. I'm calling 911. Are you shot?" I said while scanning his body and the ground around him for signs of blood.

"Yeah, but it hit my vest. I think I broke a couple of ribs."

I felt his chest again, and the body armor was now evident. "Thank God," I repeated as tears streamed down my face. "I don't know what I would have done if something had happened to you. Did Ted shoot you? How could he have? I saw him leave to the east."

"Not Ted. Amber," he gasped, pushing out the words. I pulled out my phone and punched 911, worried that a rib had punctured his lung.

"10-13, officer down in Strawberry Fields," I said, choking back my tears.

❖

Chapter 25 – The Reckoning

I paced in the ER waiting room at St. Luke's Roosevelt while waiting for an update on Finn. Sergeant Porter from the NYPD Central Park precinct waited patiently with me. He had notified the Bell Harbor Chief of Police once I told them that Finn was a detective there and a former detective in the NYPD. I knew that would get him to the head of the line for treatment and that's all I cared about. I'd worry about any trouble we may be in once I knew that Finn was safe.

It wasn't too long before the doctor came out to report two broken ribs but no punctured lung. The vest had saved him, but he took a good hit to the chest. Sergeant Porter planted both hands on his thighs and stood, turning toward me, saying, "Go tell Detective Finnegan to take care and that you'll see him later. I need you to come back to the Station House with me now so I can get your statement."

"Yes, sir," I said, standing and following the doctor into Finn's room. I went to his side and leaned in to hug him, recoiling as he winced. "I'm so sorry; I didn't mean to hurt you."

"I'm okay," he said. "I'm happy you're okay too."

"I don't even want to think about what could have happened if you hadn't been wearing your vest."

"Yeah, we all complain about them, but we aren't dumb enough to respond to a job without them. I still wish you would have worn one, but get why you couldn't."

"I have to go with Sergeant Porter back to his precinct in Central Park and give a statement. Will you be okay? What did the doctor tell you?"

"They're keeping me overnight, but I'll get released in the morning. I wish I could go with you, but I'll give my statement tomorrow. Will you be alright by yourself?"

"Yeah, Sergeant Porter is with me, and I'll go stay with my parents tonight. I'll meet you here in the morning."

"Did they catch her yet?"

"Not that I know of, but they will. She's not known for her brilliance," I said, trying to smile, but it fell flat. "Did I get this all wrong? Was it Amber the whole time? Was I so focused on Ted that I missed what was really going on, and it got you shot?"

"Don't go there. Let the police take it from here. They'll find her. You go with the sergeant and text me when you get to your parents' home safely."

I leaned carefully over him and kissed his forehead. I lingered and whispered, "Thank God you're okay, Finn. When I thought I had lost you, I... I... I just don't know what I would have done."

"You can't get rid of me that easily," he said and smiled as I pulled back. "I'm alright. You go with Porter and keep checking in, okay?"

"Okay," I smiled and turned to find the sergeant.

***

The precinct had that worn look that is hard to find anywhere other than a busy police station - or "house," as the NYPD affectionately calls them. This one was unique as it sat in the middle of Central Park.

It was small but boasted adjacent stables for the elegant and powerful NYPD horses that patrol the park. Upon entry, you are met with a high desk where the Desk Sergeant stands guard over the activity at the front. Porter escorted me past the fortified wall and into the depths of the building.

Down a poorly lit hall, we entered a room with at least a dozen desks paired off, each anchored by an out-of-date computer monitor and overflowing in/out box. Heads turned as we walked in, and Porter announced, "witness to the Strawberry Fields shooting," and motioned me towards an unused desk. I sat, and he pulled out Form 61 - the standard form for filing a criminal complaint in New York City.

"You know the drill, right? Heard you used to be a D.A. in the Bronx," he said.

"Yeah, but that was a lifetime ago. Ask anything you need."

"Roger that."

Together, we completed the biographical section, and then he asked me to recite what happened for the official statement. I paused, wondering where to start. I began at the beginning, explaining the circuitous route that I took in the investigation. Porter was quiet, listening, occasionally prodding for more detail. When I was done, I pulled my phone from my purse and pushed it across the desk to him, adding, "And I recorded the meeting."

He took my phone placing it next to his legal pad on which he had taken notes while I spoke. He glanced across the page and then, while tapping his pen on the pad, said, "That's quite a story." He leaned back in his swivel chair, and for a moment, I worried it would give under him. Eventually, he pulled himself upright, saying, "You realize you put yourself in a lot of danger setting that trap for your ex, right?"

"I do now. I didn't think Amber was involved, so I figured the danger might come afterward, not in the park. I'm lucky Finn was with me, but I feel awful that he was shot."

"Yeah, he's one lucky SOB. Could have been a lot worse. I've got your statement, and I'd ask that you send me that recording, please," he said as he handed me back my phone and a business card. "We'll talk to Detective Finnegan in the morning for his version of events. In the meantime, we have the suspect's name and description. There's an APB out for her. We should have her in custody shortly."

"And what about Ted?"

"Well, he didn't break any laws in New York as far as I can see. We've got nothing to pick him up on. Should we find out he was involved, in any way, with the shooting, that will change. But for now, he's a free man."

"Should I be scared?" I asked.

"Amber's more worried about saving herself now than coming after you. And we don't know that Ted was involved with this attempt to shoot you. But I'll have an RMP take you home and park outside tonight. Would that work?" The RMP lingo flooded back from my days working with the NYPD - Radio, Motor, Patrol car. How could I ever forget?

"That would be great. I'm staying with my parents over on West 71st. The marked car outside tonight should do a lot to scare her off if she shows up. Thank you."

"No problem."

Two officers drove me to the West Side. I rode in the back trying not to touch anything and planning a thorough hand wash once inside my parent's house. I tried not to imagine the fluids and germs that were potentially riding along with me. The officers opened my door, escorted me up the steps, and waited until my mother answered the bell. She offered them something to drink and snacks and was undeterred by their polite refusals.

"Don't be silly," she said as she waved them inside. "It'll just take a second." My mother was a proper Southern lady, no matter how long she had lived in New York City. She got her way every time and would hear of nothing else. She hurried back to her kitchen to fetch what I assumed to be a picnic of sorts when the officers' radios crackled to life. "Car 15 report in. Sarge wants to talk to you."

"Tell your mom sorry, we've got to get back to the car," the taller one said.

"No worries," I replied and closed and locked the door behind them. My father, who had hung back to watch the activity of my arrival, was anxious for an update on the day's events so I promised the full tale in the morning in return for sleep now. Before I went up to bed, I walked back and gave my mom the news that her picnic had been canceled and then went up to their guest room to fall into bed after a hell of a day.

I still couldn't quite believe that the shooter was Amber. I guess it all made sense. She was desperate to get out of Texas and her nightmarish life. Her criminal profile indicated she would do anything to survive. She had dropped out of high school, lived in a run-down weekly motel, stripped and God knows what else at the Brass Ass, and then found her ticket out - my husband at the time. What would she do to hold onto him? To the life he enabled for her? Was killing someone too much to believe?

Not really, when I thought about her circumstances. I had never credited her with much but I did believe in her desire to survive. I hope they catch her soon; I thought as I fell asleep and smiled, knowing with certainty that my mother was currently delivering a full picnic to two NYPD officers in their RMP on West 71st Street.

***

I woke before dawn after having tossed and turned all night. I quickly showered and pulled on my clothes from the day before (noting that my mother had, at some point during my sleep, collected them and washed them) and quietly tiptoed downstairs. I opened the front door to retrieve the newspaper and check on our overnight sentries.

The morning sun was now out, and it shone in a clear blue sky that you only get on crisp winter days. I pulled my jacket around me, approached their car window, and knocked, trying not to startle them. The officer in the passenger seat lowered her window and I offered to bring them back coffee from the deli I was headed to on the corner. They thanked me for the offer and agreed I could go unescorted because they could see my whole route. I returned with not only coffee but egg and cheese sandwiches to a hearty thanks and then headed back inside with my own breakfast.

It was approaching eight when my parents joined me in the kitchen, and over coffee and more egg sandwiches from my earlier breakfast run, I talked them through the events of the previous day. My mother busied herself interrupting and offering advice on what I could have done differently, while my father alternated between actively listening and shushing my mother. In the end, I got through the recitation with only mild negative feedback on my execution of the plan but plentiful shock and finger wagging at the danger of the larger situation and the shooting. I apologized for the thousandth time for bringing Ted into our lives and all his chaos with him. They commiserated with me and invited me to stay at their home until everything was resolved.

I declined, saying, "I really appreciate your offer, but I need to get back to my home, my students, and Pumpkin. I'll be okay, I promise." I stood, clearing our dishes into the kitchen and throwing out the sandwich wrappers. I thanked my parents again, giving them each a hug and peck on the cheek, and then headed out to inform the police officers of my plans to walk down to St. Luke's, which was just ten blocks away.

After some negotiations about my safety, they drove me down to the hospital and accompanied me up to Finn's room. As we arrived, Finn was completing the paperwork for his release. I got to hear the doctor's directions including no strenuous activity or heavy lifting for a month to let his ribs heal.

Finn agreed, understanding that the restrictions would limit him to desk duty for him for a while and signed the forms. The officers took us straight to the Central Park precinct, where I cooled my heels with the Desk Sergeant while Finn went in back to give his statement. After about an hour, the desk phone rang, and the sergeant gruffly told me to head back to Sergeant Porter's desk. I did so and was waved into a conference room where Finn already sat at a beat-up rectangular wooden table with four chairs around it. I took the seat next to Finn, and Porter sat across from me as a female officer joined him.

"I'm Detective Walker," she said. "I'm running the attempted murder case. We have Amber Knotten in custody. We picked her up in the apartment building they used to live in on 57th Street. She was hiding out with former neighbors."

"Wow, that was fast," I commented.

"Not really," replied Walker. "It's a small island for most folks. They hide where they're comfortable."

"Is she talking?" asked Finn.

"Not yet," said Walker. "She asked to call a lawyer. So, we're in a hold position until they speak. I've notified the D.A.'s office so they have an A.D.A. ready in case she decides to talk and go for a deal."

"Anything else you need from us?" asked Finn.

"Not at this time, Detective. We'll let you and Ms. Glass know if we do."

We thanked the officers and then headed out to grab a taxi and make our way to Grand Central for a train home. I was dying to get on the train and finally be able to fully debrief with Finn about my meeting with Ted in the park. With all of the chaos after the shooting, the original plan had fallen away, and now we were focused on Amber. I wasn't sure how our original plan would play out, but I was eager for Finn's thoughts.

❖

Chapter 26 – The Prints

Once back in Bell Harbor, we went straight to the police station and Finn carefully extracted the file out of my tote with gloved hands. He slid it into an evidence bag, marked it with relevant details, and taped and signed it for chain of custody. He then had the Desk Sergeant print me and submitted the file, including Amber's print card shared by the NYPD, and my elimination prints, to their lab with a "rush" designation. I then headed home, and Finn dutifully reported to his Chief's office for what we were both certain, was going to be a barrel full of trouble.

I swung by Grounded on my way home to thank Megan for staying the night with Pumpkin. She provided a Chai Soy Latte in return for a full recap of the New York City events. After I had gone through the timeline, we both sat contemplating the full story.

"She's crazy as a shithouse rat, as my relatives in the south used to say," I summarized with a shrug.

"You could say that again," nodded Megan.

"Desperate people can do just about anything to maintain what they have. She came from nothing and finally tasted what it's like to have everything - at least 'everything' by her definition. Although to be honest, I have always thought that her definition of 'everything', and that of my ex, is pretty empty sounding. They think happiness is fancy clothes, cars, vacations, and meals. None of it centers on the people in their lives or the difference they can make in the lives of others."

"To me, it all sounds rather sad. To feel so insecure that you need stuff to feel important," added Megan.

"Yeah. I've always worried that my kids would pick up some of that materialism. I try and counter it with lots of family time when they're with me but I think I come across as rather boring compared to a dad who buys them anything they want."

"Someday, they'll see him for who he really is," consoled Megan.

"I used to think that, but I don't anymore; he's gotten away with too much. At least now Amber will be out of the picture. She was a horrible influence, especially on my girls. All she ever talked about was dieting, fashion, make-up, and skincare to avoid aging. I always wanted her gone; I just never thought it would be like this. Jeez. It still feels unreal. Can you believe she shot Finn?"

"Thank God Finn is okay. Think of all that's happened in just the last 24 hours! Go home. Hug Pumpkin. Take a long soak in the tub. Drink a cup of hot tea. I'll stop by after we close."

I thanked her with a long hug and drove up Nutmeg Hill, lost in my thoughts. I did just as she suggested after getting home. Pumpkin welcomed me with enthusiasm and we snuggled on the couch with lots of belly scratches until she calmed down. I walked to the kitchen and boiled water for tea and then carried the steaming mug with me to the bath. I ran the hot water and peeled off my clothes, dropping them in a pile while telling Pumpkin about all she had missed.

When it was full, and my bubbles added, I sank into the suds, allowing the heat to melt away my stress and anxiety. I sipped my tea and then lowered myself, dunking my hair so the water held it back out of my eyes when I came up. I let my feet float to the top, and my mind roamed across the past day as the events replayed again, like a movie.

Pumpkin's bark brought me back from my daydream as she sat up with her ears alert.

"What is it, girl?" I asked. "Go see," I directed. Probably Megan, I thought, noting that I had let the time get away from me, as usual, when I took a bath. Pumpkin trotted out of the bathroom and I sank under the water once more and then began to use the hand sprayer to rinse myself of bubbles.

Two hands gripped my shoulders from the back and pushed me under the water. I kicked and flailed but slipped against the still-soapy rim of the tub. I don't want to die, was all I could think. I pushed both my feet flat against the end of the tub at the curve for some resistance, tightened my core, and swung the hand sprayer with all my force back behind my head. I hit something, and the hands loosened enough that I sat up gasping for air and turned, still swinging.

Ted was over me, his face contorted in hate, raging, "You bitch!" He tried to grab at me again, but the slippery suds helped, and I twisted out of his reach and held onto the faucet, pulling myself away from him and over the side of the tub to the floor. He lunged at me and was on top of me before I could scramble away, choking me before I could get up.

I reached my arms up, flailing for anything I could use to defend myself. I grabbed for the scale with both hands and brought it over his head with a horrible thud. He dropped, falling onto me, and I pushed him off and crawled away. I grabbed a towel and ran, dripping, to the front of the house, out the front door, and straight into

Finn's arms.

"What's going on?" he said in alarm.

"Ted's in there; he attacked me in the tub. I think I knocked him out, but I don't know." I gasped for air more from adrenaline than anything else. "And Pumpkin! Where's Pumpkin? She went to protect me." Finn took off his coat, wrapped me in it, and pulled his weapon.

"Is he armed?"

"Not that I saw."

He took out his cell phone and called for backup, telling me to stay put and went into the house, methodically clearing each room and corner as he went. A few short minutes later, which felt like hours, Finn appeared with a cuffed and bleeding Ted.

Back-up arrived simultaneously, as did an ambulance. I ran inside, searching for my dog, finding her bleeding with one of my kitchen knives next to her on the floor. It looked like Ted had stabbed her halfway down her back. I grabbed a dish towel and pressed it to the wound, screaming for help.

Finn and others came running, and a uniformed police officer carried Pumpkin out to the backseat of his cruiser. He promised to speed her to the emergency vet clinic, and I told him I'd meet them there.

I ran back inside, threw on yoga pants and an old Colby sweatshirt, and pulled my curls up into a clip. Once back outside, I was stopped by the paramedics. I declined treatment for myself, signing papers to that effect, and the ambulance took my bleeding ex-husband away, followed by a police car. I ran to my car, yelling to Finn over my shoulder that I'd be back as soon as I checked on Pumpkin.

When I got to the vet clinic, Pumpkin was already inside and under care. The police officer who brought her in had waited and told me the vet had said she was stable but needed blood, fluids, and stitches. I paced until a nurse came out and repeated the same information to me and the officer who had kindly continued to wait with me. She told me Pumpkin had been lucky; the stab wound had missed all her vital organs.

The wound had been cleaned and closed, and Pumpkin was sedated and sleeping. She let me go in to see her. Pumpkin lay on a gurney with an IV coming out of her front paw and was asleep. I gingerly leaned in to hug her and rubbed my face in the velvety nook behind her ear, whispering how much I loved her and how brave she was.

I thanked her for protecting me and left her asleep on the bed. The nurse said I could come back in the morning for a visit, and they would take good care of her. With that, the police officer followed me back home to face the chaos I had left.

Crime Scene personnel still busied themselves at the kitchen door, which I supposed was the point of entry and my bathroom. I also saw remnants of fingerprint dust across other surfaces throughout my home and sighed at the cleaning ahead of me. I was still in a stupor of disbelief at what had occurred when Finn found me and hugged me to him. I breathed in his scent of sandalwood and soap and tried to use the moment to calm myself. How could this have happened? I wondered again.

Finn led me to my couch and sat me down to give my statement. I took him and Officer DeCarlo through the events and answered their questions that punctuated my tale as best I could. Finally, Finn patted my knee, saying, "That's enough for now." DeCarlo nodded in agreement, stowing the complaint paperwork in a folder and making his way out my front door.

I curled up on the couch, waiting for the tide of people to ebb, which it did relatively quickly. Once the scene was clear and we were alone, Finn came inside again to join me. He hugged me, and I began to weep. I cried over all that had happened and all that had changed for me and my kids, and with relief that this nightmare was finally over.

A short time later, Megan arrived in a panic after seeing the crime scene tape still fluttering outside, and joined in a three-way hug after hearing Finn's quick rendition of events.

"My God, you're lucky," she said, hugging me again.

"I don't feel lucky right now," I quipped, trying to smile.

"You know what I meant," she smiled.

Eventually, we sat on the couch together with wine and the pizza Megan had brought for dinner. Surrounded by the two of them, my mood had shifted from shock at Ted's attack, to relief that perhaps it was all, finally, over.

"Well, there's a twist I didn't see coming," said Megan.

"I'll second that," I added.

When Finn didn't add to our chatter, Megan and I turned to him. "Well, Mr. tall, dark and mysterious, something we should know?" I asked.

"The fingerprints were Ted's."

"Which ones?" Megan and I asked in unison.

"Both sets of them. Texas and your storage locker. That's what I was on my way to tell you when you came running out into the street earlier."

"Wait, what does that mean? I thought Amber was the killer because she shot at me. Now we're saying it was Ted in Texas?" I looked at Megan, who shook her head in confusion.

"Maybe," said Finn. "Or, Amber is the killer, and Ted is the fixer. Either way, we've got him dead to rights. I called the prosecutor in Texas and the Yale defense team. Croft will certainly get a new trial now. I'm not sure the fingerprints would have been enough on their own, but Amber and Ted's behavior over the last day is enough to call everything into question, I'd say."

"Woohoo!" cheered Megan. "We did it. We cleared Croft." She high-fived Finn and then me.

"Finn," I started, "they have Amber in custody in New York, and you have Ted here. I'm assuming Texas will want to speak to Ted, too? Will they come here, or will they seek extradition?"

"Probably come here to interview him first, and then, if they feel they have enough, they'll seek to extradite. They may also seek the same through New York for Amber if they find evidence of her involvement in Tiffany's death. I'll interview Ted first thing in the morning. Tonight, he's getting medical care. So, we'll know more tomorrow."

"I don't know what I thought would happen when all this began but I certainly didn't think it would end with both of them under arrest. I had no idea either of them was capable of this." I paused, reflecting on what I had said, and then continued, "Or maybe I just didn't want to believe they could be."

"I blame myself," said Finn, shaking his head. "I never should have let you go meet Ted. That escalated all of this and nearly got you killed."

"Now you listen to me," I said grabbing his arms and squaring him to face me. "You didn't let me do anything. I'm a grown woman and make my own decisions. I would have gone to that meeting with or without you. You saved my life by engaging Amber and got yourself shot in the process. I'll be forever grateful to you."

We hugged and then settled back into the couch.

"Have you told your kids yet?" asked Megan.

"I know I need to call them, but I'm dreading it. I don't want them to hear about any of this from anyone else though. Honestly, I'm not sure what I'll say to them."

"What you've always said to them, the truth," suggested Megan.

"Yeah, but this truth is hard. The girls especially have resisted believing who their dad really is all these years. This will be a shock."

"It's a shock no matter what, and you can't keep protecting them from him. This is a Band-Aid you need to rip off quickly," counseled Finn.

"Okay," I said, rising. "Then I'd better get to it."

Finn and Megan stood, clearing their plates and glasses into the kitchen, and putting the leftovers in my fridge. Megan bear hugged me goodbye, pushing the air out of me, and Finn gently kissed my lips, asking me to call him later as they both left.

I took in a deep breath and exhaled tucking my feet under myself on the couch as I initiated a joint FaceTime call to my kids. Both their father and stepmother had been arrested for attempted murder in the last day and I was one of the targets; there was no good way to convey that message.

Once on the call with the three of them, I kept to the facts and tried to answer the barrage of questions they had as best I could. They cried and worried for their father and stepmother, and I tried to be as sympathetic as I could. They also expressed concern for me and Pumpkin and relief that we were both okay. I understood all of it, their swirl of conflicting emotions, as I had felt the same throughout the investigation.

At the same time, I knew it all wasn't nearly as hard on me as it was on them. I tried to share as many facts as I knew but they had far more questions than I had answers.

I told them we'd know more tomorrow after the police interviewed Ted and Amber, and we could go from there. I promised an update call the next evening and told them again how sorry I was. I debated telling them about Steve Croft but decided I had said enough for one night, and, after all, I didn't have any facts to share on that case yet.

I wondered about Croft. If not for him, would my conflicting emotions and the continuing need to protect my kids have stopped me from investigating his case further? But deep down, I knew I needed to know who Ted really was. I needed to understand all that had happened in our marriage and my life.

When I was honest with myself, I knew that I had to figure this out for myself. Up until now, all my decisions had been driven by the needs of my kids. The decision to pursue this case had been for me. As a mother, I wondered if that was selfish, but the inner voice of Maggie had gotten stronger in Bell Harbor, and I had listened to her.

We continued to talk and cried together until there wasn't more to say and hung up with "I love you" all around. I crawled into bed feeling totally alone and remembering a sign that used to hang in my office, "Sometimes the right thing and the hardest thing are the same." Cold comfort tonight.

❖

Chapter 27 – Blame

Finn let me watch Ted's interview from behind the two-way glass. They sat in chairs facing one another in a dingy room with an old table bolted to the floor between them. Ted sat back in his chair, legs extended and crossed at the ankles as though already bored. His lawyer, a young man in an expensive gray, chalk-striped suit, leaned forward, taking notes and occasionally placing his hand on Ted's arm to stop him from speaking.

Finn asked basic questions on his whereabouts yesterday and Ted seemed to be admitting most of the elements which placed him in Connecticut and at my home. But both he and his lawyer seemed confident. Their confidence worried me; I had seen this confidence in Ted before, and it had never ended well for me.

And then Ted said, "I was invited into her home to discuss some family matters, and my crazy ex-wife attacked me. She hit me over the head with something when I looked away."

His lawyer quickly added, "It's a 'he said, she said' case, no proof either way."

"And what about the dog?" asked Finn. "I suppose she attacked you for no reason, too?"

"Nah, Maggie trained her to hate me, just like she tried to do with our kids. She's a bitch and won't be happy until she ruins my life."

"That seems a bit dramatic, Mr. Melody. Don't you think?" commented Finn.

"Look where I am," replied Ted. "I wouldn't say it's so dramatic anymore, would you?"

Finn paused, shuffling papers and then pivoted to ask about the fires, focusing first on my storage locker where Ted's print was found. Ted feigned surprise at the fires, but Finn countered with Ted's statements to me in Central Park, admitting that he knew about them.

"My kids told me, so what?" Ted countered.

"So what? Well, how do you explain your prints being present in your ex-wife's storage locker?"

"Don't answer that," interrupted his lawyer.

"Why not?" said Ted, "Why wouldn't my fingerprints still be on some of my ex's stuff? We were married for over a decade." He smiled, uncrossing and then re-crossing his legs as if fully relaxed. "I've seen enough *Law & Order* to know you can't date a fingerprint." He smiled again and winked at Finn.

Finn stood and excused himself and, a moment later, entered the observation room with me.

"When did you get the exercise bike that his print was on?' he asked.

"It was my parents' hand-me-down, and they gave it to me during our marriage. But it was cleaned and wiped down regularly; no way his print survived fifteen years on that bike. Right?"

"Probably, but it's enough of a question to have them argue it, and maybe successfully," he said.

"He's talking his way out of everything, isn't he?" I asked, fighting back the tears welling in my eyes.

"No, we still have the Texas print. That's harder for him to wiggle out of."

"Are you going to ask about it?"

"Not my place, need to wait for the Texas Ranger, he's on his way. Should be here this afternoon."

I exhaled. My ex had always been like Teflon, with accountability easily slipping off of him. He had slithered through our divorce trial owing minimal child support, bypassed a criminal contempt conviction after the civil court failed to register it with criminal authorities, and slipped away from his ongoing behavior by lying to our kids about it with enough panache that they believed him.

"He'll get away with it all. He always does," I said, visibly deflating.

Finn grabbed my shoulders and looked me in the eye, "not this time. I promise." He pulled me to him, and we clung to each other in the cramped room.

After leaving the police station, I went straight to the vet clinic to check on Pumpkin and found she had slept well and would be ready for release in a couple of days. The vet wanted her to stay longer in order to keep her slightly sedated so she would stay still and heal. I smiled because they clearly didn't realize how much she regularly napped during the day, but I was glad for their attentive care of her. They let me visit with her once I promised not to excite her. I nuzzled in her neck and thanked her again for protecting me. I encouraged her to sleep and rest and told her I'd be back the next day to check on her.

As I was leaving, her eyes were already fluttering back to sleep.

I went home and graded papers, trying to catch up with the classwork I had been neglecting. Finn texted updates throughout the afternoon as the Ranger had arrived and was talking to Ted. The short summaries I got from Finn were not encouraging. Ted was in a state of full denial and explained away the Texas fingerprint, saying he was a club regular. By dinner time, Finn texted that the Ranger had asked to continue his questioning of Ted the following day and was headed down to the city to speak to Amber. Finn promised further updates as he got them but was equally buried in work he had put off over the last couple of days.

I had a wildly unproductive evening. I read and re-read student essays and found myself pacing, rather than sitting and trying to focus. This was my worst nightmare. If Ted talked himself out of everything, then my children would blame me and maybe even believe I had made it all up - exactly what their father had always told them about me. I had promised to call them with an update. I dialed into the family FaceTime and shared the few facts I had learned that day. I let them know their dad had a lawyer, and so far, although a criminal complaint had been drafted, no indictments had moved forward - so no charges were filed.

They asked about Amber, and on that point, I had no updates other than that a Texas Ranger was talking to both of them about a ten-year-old crime that had occurred outside Dallas. That had Carter perk up and ask about that crime. I told them a man had been convicted of arson and murder at the strip club where Amber had worked and that he was on death row and nearing his execution. I added that the

Ranger was here to make sure their dad and stepmom didn't know any more about the crime than they had told authorities at the time. That gave all the kids pause.

"Texas police are in Connecticut to talk to dad? That's really serious, isn't it? I mean, they wouldn't come all that way-" Ruby broke off, beginning to cry.

"I'm not gonna lie. Yes, this is serious. But at this point, they are just talking; it's too early to know what will come of all this," I said.

Carter and Meryl were both studiously quiet. I couldn't read the range of emotions that were flooding my children's faces. They were clearly worried about where all of this could go. I reassured them as best I could but was also worried about what was to come and told them so. I said we needed to trust the police to do their jobs. We ended a call that left more questions than answers for all of us. I told them all I loved them and got murmurs of the same in return. I cried myself to sleep that night as I felt my children slipping away from me.

Chapter 28 – Hail Mary

After another night of restless sleep, I visited Pumpkin first thing in the morning, and she was healing well and able to come home in another day. I counted that blessing and returned home to try and get some classwork done.

Finn called a little after lunch and caught me in my home office trying to ignore the case and focus on my student essays again, to little success.

"Any news?" I jumped in before he even said hello.

"Impatient much?" he joked. "Yes, the mudslinging has begun."

"What does that mean?"

"The Ranger came and questioned Ted and then went down and spoke to Amber. Amber denied Ted's involvement until she heard that he threw her under the bus. What is it they say? No honor among thieves? Anyways, she now says she was acting on Ted's directions in the park, and Ted says she acted alone. He called her a 'crazy bitch who's stupid as a rock'. Either way, she's going down, and if she can provide any substantiation of Ted's involvement, he will too, at least for my shooting and the attempt on you."

"What about Texas?" I prodded.

"Same dance there. He blames her for Tiffany's death but denies knowing any detail and dismisses his print as innocent at a club that he frequented. It's like he's trying to sink her. He didn't need to give her up for the Texas murder; he could have just denied everything for both of them. She claimed ignorance of everything until she heard he blamed her. She says Tiffany's death was an innocent accident - that she and Ted were arguing, and Tiffany tripped and fell, hitting her head on the way down. She says he covered it all up with the fire. Her testimony plus the print on him is a very weak case; I'm not gonna lie to you."

"I know it is. Testimony of a co-conspirator needs corroboration to be admissible. We need more."

"Yeah, but Amber is no brain surgeon. She doesn't offer a lot, and it seems Ted really exploited that over the years. My gut is that she did a lot she didn't think up on her own and maybe didn't even understand at the time it was happening."

"I bet she's looking back on her time with Ted now just like I did. Replaying everything that happened through a new, clearer lens."

"Yeah, you've both been taken by the guy. He's a real manipulator."

"Hey," I said. "That gives me an idea. Could I talk to her?"

"Seriously, Maggie? What good would that do?"

"We've both been screwed over by the same crappy guy. Maybe I can work that angle to find out more."

Finn paused.

"Let me ask," he finally said and hung up.

***

An hour later, Finn and I were on the Metro North, speeding south. Finn put his hand on my thigh to stop my nervous toe-tapping.

245

"It'll be okay," he whispered.

"No, it won't, and you know it. I need to get her talking."

"This isn't all on you, Maggie. The NYPD and Rangers both took a crack at her and didn't get anything on him. No one expects anything from you; this is a Hail Mary."

"Wow, thanks for the vote of confidence." I elbowed him and immediately regretted it as he cringed from the knock to the ribs.

"I'm so sorry! I forgot."

"No worries. I'm healing. No thanks to you," he added with a wink.

"Oh, Finn, I'm so sorry," I said and gently rubbed his chest. He kissed me to let me know all was forgiven. I kissed back, to be far away from what I was about to do, if only for a moment.

We spent the rest of the journey strategizing about my talk with Amber. The biggest obstacle I could see was that she hated me and certainly didn't trust me. Ted had spent their entire time together telling her what a shrew I was.

The advantage I had was her basic thirst for survival. Her criminal profile showed she was willing to do anything to survive. She had run away from an abusive father, stripped, lived in a by-the-week motel, clung on to the first man willing to get her out, and tried to kill me when I threatened her hard-won lifestyle. Had she done even more than that? If I gave her a rope, perhaps she would see it as a lifeline to save herself, and I could use it to hang her. At least, that was the hope.

***

I walked into the interview room, and Amber looked up, "Oh hell no." She protested, pushing back from the table.

"Take a seat and listen," said Finn, shoving her back down to sitting.

I sat across from her and began, "You can leave, Detective. Let Amber and me talk alone, please."

Finn left, and Amber sat back in her chair, her long arms and legs both crossed in a position of pure defiance. Her normally carefully coifed hair was pulled back in a disheveled ponytail, and her regularly plumped face had begun to deflate, revealing her age as nearer to mine than she'd like to admit. With the lipstick off the pig, she looked like the runaway who became a stripper, not the socialite persona she had conjured out of thin air for her life with Ted and my kids. I felt sorry for her all over again. She was the definition of pathetic.

"I'm sorry this is all happening, Amber."

"No, you're not, you bitch. You've wished this on me since we first met."

"This isn't about me, Amber. I'm not doing this to you. This is all Ted."

"Bullshit. You set us up."

"Hardly. Ted has blamed you for everything, including the murder in Texas and the shooting of the detective in Central Park. If you don't stand up for yourself soon, he'll walk away from this straight into the arms of another woman, and you'll be locked up forever."

"He'd never do that to me. He loves me."

"Yeah, he's very convincing at that. I know first-hand. The first year of our marriage he wrote me love poetry and kept a fresh rose on my nightstand that he replaced every week. While he was sneaking around with you, he was slow dancing with me in our living room after we put the kids to bed. We were planning the rest of our lives together. I loved him, Amber, and I thought he loved me. But I was wrong."

"Yeah, cuz he loves me."

"No, because he is a sociopath and incapable of loving anyone but himself. At the beginning of our break-up, we got joint counseling. He was diagnosed as a sociopath. I asked the therapist what that meant, and she said he doesn't have the ability to have emotions - he can't love me, our kids, you, or anyone else. It's a personality disorder that can't be fixed. She told me I had to divorce him."

"He said that's a lie. You've tried to poison the kids against him for years with that lie - it never worked."

"It's not a lie, and you know it, Amber. He showed you who he really was far more than he ever showed me, didn't he? He felt safe enough with you to be himself like he never could with me. Who knows, maybe what you two had was a kind of love for him."

She didn't respond, so I pressed on. "At the strip clubs, and with the deals to move the money through the clubs, he was himself. With me, he was pretending all the time. But I bet you've noticed him changing over the years, haven't you? He travels more, even weekends sometimes, right? Does he miss birthdays and other big occasions? He still buys you things, but they aren't thoughtful anymore; they're flashy. Once he moved you in with him, he was gone more and left you on babysitting duty, didn't he?"

"We have a great life together. We have everything," she countered.

"Didn't he promise you a fancy wedding and a big party to celebrate your love? Never happened, did it?"

"We didn't need that to prove our love for one another," she said with her bottom lip pouting. "It was romantic at the justice of the peace."

"But you wanted it, didn't you? Bet he said he couldn't afford it. Wasn't there always an excuse for why it couldn't happen?"

She stared down at her hands on the table and didn't respond, so I kept on. "I know how he is because he did that to me. He promised me the world, too. I was going back to school to be an architect. That had always been my dream since I was a little girl. He encouraged me to enroll and take a full semester of classes. My second semester he said we couldn't afford it anymore, and if I loved our family, I needed to slow down the pace so it would be cheaper each semester. Of course, I immediately withdrew from many of my classes. I found out during the divorce that it was all a lie. We had plenty of money. He was diverting it to other accounts, so I couldn't see it, and he was spending it on you and other women."

"He told me you couldn't cut it in school and failed out," she mumbled without looking up.

"You know that's not true, don't you, Amber? I understand how much you want to believe everything he says. I did, too. But he doesn't care about either one of us. He has tried to ruin my life for a long time, don't let him ruin yours too. Even if you somehow get out of this, he'll never take you back."

"Yes, he will," she said confidently. "He always will."

"No, he won't; he's saving himself and throwing you under the bus. He's already talked to the Texas Rangers about what you did to Tiffany."

"He knows better than that."

"I don't think so, Amber. He gave statements to Texas, Connecticut, and New York. The life you had is over; he's cutting ties with you. The only reason I'm here is that I am the only one who really knows what a liar he is. The police don't believe you when you blame him, but I do."

"What's in it for you? Why should I believe you'd want to help me?" She picked at her cuticle, which was already raw.

"You're right; I don't care about what happens to you. But I'm sick of Ted getting away with everything. He lies so easily and everyone always believes him. I never got any justice for everything he did to me and my kids, but you still can. If there's anything you have to corroborate your story - I mean to prove it - then they'll believe you instead of him. If not, you'll go to jail for the rest of your life. And that jail will likely be in Texas."

"Not Texas!" she recoiled at the thought. "I can't go back there. I swore I would never go back after I got out."

"Well, that's where Ted is sending you."

"He can't; I can prove I didn't kill Tiffany."

"Yeah, you told them it was an accident, right?"

"No," she said and paused. "I mean, I can prove it wasn't an accident, and it wasn't me. If I can prove that they won't send me back there, will they?"

"Nope. If you weren't involved in the Texas killing, you wouldn't be sent back."

"I have the paperweight."

"Is that what killed Tiffany?"

"Yeah. Her blood and stuff were still on it, and while he started the fire, I picked it up with a scarf and dropped it in my purse. I kept it all these years just in case he tried to throw me over for a newer model. He thinks I'm stupid, but I'm not."

"No, you're not, Amber. I don't think he gave you enough credit. But he will now. Why did he kill her?"

"She wanted a cut of the money we were making in the VIP room to fund her habit. She was a fool. I told her he'd never go for it, but she confronted him anyway. Said she'd go to the cops unless he cut her in. There was so much money I don't know why he had to do it. She was the only real friend I'd ever had. I figured the paperweight might come in handy someday."

"And it has. Where is it now?"

"In a safety deposit box in Dallas. I was scared to keep a key in case he ever found it, so it's a code. My birthday plus the day I ran away from home."

"Okay, I'm sure the police will want all that. Do you have any proof he told you what to do in Central Park?"

"No. He said I should shoot you, and they'd just assume it was random violence in New York."

"Where did you get the gun?"

"We've had one for use in the clubs, you know, just in case. Ted got it, but I don't know where."

"How'd you learn to shoot?"

"My grandaddy taught me. I used to spend time at their house to be away from my daddy. Grandaddy taught me to shoot at tin cans on their fence." Her look seemed far away as she remembered.

"Do you still have the gun?"

"Nah, I stashed it."

"Where?"

"In the planter in the lobby of our old building on 57th. There's a big urn that holds a smaller potted plant; I just slipped it down the side."

"Why did he burn my storage locker and car? After all, that's what started all of this for me."

"When you posted on my Instagram page about having proof about the Brass Ass, some of his investors flipped out. They told him to shut you up. He figured if there was no proof, you'd be done. The kids said you had a storage locker where you kept all the divorce paperwork. Plus, I heard you talk to them once on the phone about everything." She had used air quotes around the word investors while rolling her eyes. She continued, adding, "He thinks I'm an airhead, but because of that, they let me hear lots of things, and I figured I might need some of it someday - so I wrote a lot of it down, even if I didn't know what it all meant. I also took pictures of some of the bank papers he had me sign. Would that help, too?"

"It sure would. If you repeat everything you've told me to the detectives, they'll be able to help you. Plus, provide them the paperweight and other evidence, of course."

"Okay, Maggie. Tell the kids I'm sorry. I didn't mean for this to blow back on them."

"You tell them, Amber. You're still their stepmom. They need to hear from you to understand how you got caught up in all of this." I paused, adding, "Have you ever told them your real story?"

"Nah, they don't need to hear that. That world is so far away from them, and it should stay there. I left it all in Texas."

"I think you should tell them. Give them credit for being able to understand what you've been through. Help them understand if they don't."

"Maybe," she said, finally looking at me dead in the eye.

I stood to leave and turned back to her, "You're doing the right thing, Amber. He doesn't love you and has turned on you. Save yourself."

"Yep. Mama didn't raise no fool," she quipped, allowing her Texas twang to surface. "Hope for the best but expect the worst of men, I guess. If the Brass Ass taught me nothing else, I sure learned that" she said without looking at me and went back to picking at her cuticle. It was like watching her regress to the frightened girl who had run away all those years ago. I'm glad she'll survive this. I don't like her and never will, but she's led a hellish life, mostly at the hands of evil men. Maybe this will finally set her free, I thought as I shut the interrogation room door behind me.

❖

Chapter 29 – Home

Finn and I took a late train home and I fell asleep against him on the ride. He woke me as we pulled into the New Haven station, and he drove us the rest of the way in his waiting car. Once home, we slept, curled around one another until dawn, both exhausted by the last few days. I woke, made coffee, and sat at the kitchen table, replaying my conversation with Amber until Finn appeared, freshly showered and dressed.

"I've got to get into the station; I'm still in the dog house with the Chief."

"Of course," I said, rising to walk him to the door.

"You'll be okay on your own?"

"Yes, absolutely. I have to go get Pumpkin soon anyway."

He kissed me on the forehead and was gone.

I showered and pulled on jeans, brown boots, and my Irish sweater and headed out to get my girl. Pumpkin's tail wagged as I helped her into her co-pilot seat. The sun shone as I drove onto the pea-gravel driveway of our home, and I thought how crazy it was that just six months before, we had driven up to this house for the first time. I sat in the car and admired the white clapboard house, its cupola with tiny stained-glass windows, and its oddly pitched roof. I loved the wrap-around porch and its generous swing. I still hoped the three bedrooms inside would host my kids and even grandkids one day.

My kids. My kids. Tears slid down my face. Had I lost them? Would they forgive the role I had played in the arrest of their dad? In the arrest of their stepmom? Had I hurt them? I wept. Every decision I have ever made since I found out I was pregnant with Carter, my oldest, was for them. I always wanted to be an example for them, not the warning their father had been. But had I done that? Oh God, had I ruined all of it by following through on this investigation? Should I have just let it all go? But I knew myself; I was the proverbial dog with a bone. There was no way Maggie Glass could have walked away from this. I had to hope my kids would understand and, eventually, forgive me. Pumpkin crawled across the seat and squeezed herself into my lap. I gulped down my tears and laughed, scratching her ears.

"I'm okay, girl. It'll all be okay." As I spoke the words, I silently prayed they were true.

I opened the car door, and we walked up the broad stairs and onto the deep porch. The *New London Chronicle* sat on my front mat. I took it inside with us and laid down fresh food and water for Pumpkin. After I made a cup of coffee for myself, I sat at the kitchen table and unfurled the paper to the above-the-fold headline and article:

Local Arson Sparks Solution to Murder in Texas

By: Daryl Messin

A suspicious fire burned at the Stor-It-All on Windham Road last October 24th, totally consuming only one locker, that of Maggie Glass. Ms. Glass is a new Bell Harbor resident and Associate Professor of Criminology at Eastern Connecticut University.

Detective Mike Finnegan of the Bell Harbor Police Department soon determined that her space had been broken into before the fire, but nothing appeared to be missing. The crime was classified as arson. Due to the blaze, forensic evidence was sparse; only a single fingerprint of the perpetrator remained. The forensics did not match any known records but did match an unknown print left at a murder scene just outside of Dallas, Texas, ten years ago.

In 2011, Tiffany Schmidt, a 32-year-old woman, was killed at a Dallas strip club called the Brass Ass, and arson destroyed most of the evidence. The club owner, Steve Croft, was convicted of the murder and arson and now sits on Texas death row. The Connecticut fingerprint match called that conviction into question, but it wasn't enough to save Mr. Croft or even re-open his case without more evidence. The police were stumped in both states. The Yale Defense Clinic had taken on Croft's death row appellate work and got involved in the Connecticut case, trying to leverage the new evidence for a stay in Croft's execution.

In a strange twist of fate, Ms. Glass recognized the name of the Texas strip club as one where her ex-husband's present wife, Amber Melody, used to dance. She also knew that her ex of fifteen years, Theodore "Ted" Melody, had been a regular patron of the club.

Ms. Glass used the odd facts of the two linked crimes as a case study with her students, and together, they and a part-time investigator in Texas, Mary Jo Barnes, began to investigate. A third fire, at Ms. Glass's Bell Harbor home in mid-February, targeted the Melody divorce paperwork. The latest arson further linked the Texas and Connecticut crimes and pointed at the potential involvement of her ex-husband and his wife. The Bell Harbor police dug into the divorce financials, working with banks under the US PATRIOT Act, which allows banks to share customer information with law enforcement if it is related to money laundering or terrorist activity. This detective work produced suspicious, large money movements across Ted Melody's numerous bank accounts both within and outside of the United States.

The police still didn't have enough to link the Melodys to any of the crimes directly. So, Ms. Glass worked with the Bell Harbor police to gather her ex-husband's fingerprints for comparison to the sole recovered print in both Texas and Connecticut. However, when Ms. Glass met with Mr. Melody in Central Park in Manhattan, Amber Melody attempted to shoot her and then shot Detective Finnegan during her escape. Mrs. Melody was arrested by the NYPD shortly thereafter on East 57th Street.

The following evening, back in Bell Harbor, Mr.

Melody broke into Ms. Glass's home and, attempted to drown her in her bathtub and stabbed her dog, Pumpkin. Ms. Glass successfully fought off her ex-husband and subdued him until the police responded. Pumpkin was given medical care and will fully recover. Not only did the police arrest Ted Melody for the attempted murder of his ex-wife and animal abuse, but also the two Connecticut arsons, as his collected prints matched both the print in our state and that collected at the Texas murder scene.

Under questioning by the NYPD, BHPD, and Texas Rangers, the Melodys turned on each other. Amber was able to produce forensic evidence definitively tying her husband to the Texas murder of Tiffany Schmidt. Amber Melody now faces two New York charges of attempted murder and Texas charges of aiding and abetting after the fact for helping cover up the Schmidt murder for all these years. Ted Melody faces two Connecticut charges of arson, one charge of attempted murder, and one charge of animal abuse. The state of Texas has already filed for extradition to their state so he can face murder charges for the homicide of Tiffany Schmidt in 2011 and the arson of the Brass Ass. New York has also filed to extradite Mr. Melody for conspiracy and attempted murder. The Department of Justice has subpoenaed his financial records as well as the aforementioned divorce paperwork and is reviewing potential federal money laundering charges against both the Melodys.

The Yale Defense Clinic released the following statement, "we are gratified that justice has finally been found for Mr. Croft, who has lost ten years of his life. We want to thank Ms. Glass and the Bell Harbor Police Department for their tireless pursuit of justice." The BHPD issued the following comment, "we are confident that justice has been served and thank Ms. Glass for her service. Bell Harbor has always been a safe place to call home and will remain that way." When asked for her response to all that she had been through, Ms. Glass said, "I'm glad it's all over. I'm relieved that Tiffany has finally found justice and am devastated by the part my ex-husband and his wife have played in all of this. I'm very grateful to the Bell Harbor Police Department and especially Detective Mike Finnegan for finally solving these cases."

With this publicity, I couldn't put it off. I started a group FaceTime call with my kids and talked them through all that had happened. For once, Carter was quiet, taking it all in while his sisters cried and intermittently shook their heads in denial of what their dad and stepmom had done. Meryl wondered aloud if there wasn't some reasonable explanation for all of it.

Ruby piped up in response, "Didn't you hear Mom? Dad tried to drown her and strangle her. He's lost his mind. And Amber, well, Amber is clearly insane too."

"Actually, I don't think she is insane, Ruby," I said. "She's desperate to save the life she worked hard to get and sees potentially slipping away. She probably views her actions more as self-defense than anything else."

We fell into silence.

Carter broke it, asking, "So where's Dad and what will happen to him now?"

"I don't know all the details, but I do know that he has a lawyer and is being held here in Bell Harbor for the attacks on me and Pumpkin, and the arsons. I understand from the newspaper article I read this morning that Texas has already filed to extradite him so he can face charges for the murder of Tiffany Schmidt down in Dallas. That means that the two states will decide which case will take priority and the order he will be tried for his crimes. My guess is that given the seriousness of the allegations in Texas, he'll go there first."

"Texas," muttered Meryl. "I went with friends to Galveston for spring break last year; it's nice down there."

"He's not going on vacation to Texas, Meryl," said Carter in exasperation, "He's going to jail in Texas. And I'm assuming if he's convicted, he could end up on death row since that's where the other guy was. Is that right, Mom?"

"I don't know, Carter. It's always a possibility in Texas, and the arson there makes the homicide a more serious one. But it'll all be up to a jury."

"What should we do?" asked Ruby.

"I think you can write to him, or visit him, or do nothing. He'll always be your father, but it's up to each one of you how you handle this. There is no right or wrong way."

"But he tried to kill you," said Carter.

"Yeah, he did and I'm just beginning to deal with that and each of you will have to come to terms with it as well. But somehow the physical attack hasn't been as hard to process for me as finding out who he really was all those years ago. I thought the heartbreak of that day would kill me. It didn't. I built a new life for myself and for you three. I'm happy now, and I think each of you are too. This is all hard and I'm sure it'll get still harder before it gets easier. But we're a family and we'll help each other through it all and then move on. Together." I smiled through tears as I looked at each of them.

"Do you think you could ever forgive him?" queried Ruby.

"Maybe, eventually, but I won't forget. I learn, each time I interact with him, more about him and how to protect us from him, but also about myself. He's taken so much from me already that allowing one more moment of anger or regret about him in my life is giving him too much power. I need, we all need, to put what he has done behind us and live our lives. That's why I moved to Bell Harbor in the first place, for a fresh start," I said with a wink and brushed the tears off my cheeks with the back of my hands.

"Too soon to talk about forgiveness," nodded Carter.

"Too soon," I agreed.

"I love you, Mom. I'm so glad you're okay," said Meryl.

"Me too," added Carter and Ruby in unison.

"I love you all so much. I wish this hadn't happened, but I know we'll get through it together. We always do."

After I hung up, I called Megan and asked if I could meet her for lunch. When it was time, I bundled up and walked down Nutmeg Hill into town. After collecting her at Grounded, we walked over to Crust, the wood-fired pizza place on the river side of Water Street. We settled into a booth and ordered a margherita pizza to share and Diet Cokes. After I updated her on Pumpkin's return home, she asked about the previous day's events.

"So, how was it facing Amber?"

"Sickening. I had successfully avoided it for over fifteen years. I always saw her as part of what destroyed my marriage but now, I just see her as pathetic."

"Don't let her off the hook; she shot at you," countered Megan.

"Oh, I'm not, believe me. I don't mean pathetic as in blameless. I mean pathetic because I see what is driving her. She is the ultimate survivalist. She clung to Ted because he got her out of Texas and then stayed with him because of the life he afforded her. She was with him all those years out of loyalty to herself."

"So, she's not as dumb as everyone claims?" Megan asked.

"Let's call her street smart," I answered. "After all, she had the forethought to keep the paperweight Ted used to kill Tiffany."

"How sad, though," commented Megan. "The whole relationship between Ted and Amber is based on what they can get from each other. Or at least what she can get from him."

I nodded in agreement as our pizza arrived. I pulled a slice over to my plate to let it cool a little before I dug in.

"Why did Ted stay with her so long? What was in it for him?" she asked.

"Good question. I've wondered the same over the years. He can't love her. The best I have been able to figure out is he travels all the time and likes someone at home to run his life. And when the kids were younger, she was a built-in babysitter. Honestly, though, I don't know. Given what she said to me at the station yesterday, I wonder if she didn't threaten him with that paperweight. Or maybe she knew too much about his business, and he was keeping his enemies close-" I trailed off, thinking and taking a big bite. "The only thing I know for sure is that it wasn't for love."

"I can't imagine living my life without love," commented Megan.

"Yeah, with all he's done to hurt me and our kids over the years, I always felt like he never faced accountability. But maybe, he already had the greatest punishment anyone could get – a life without knowing the joy of love."

Megan nodded while sipping her soda and then asked, "how are the kids doing with all this?"

"About as you'd expect," I answered. "Struggling with disbelief, loyalty to their dad and stepmom, anger, shock, you name it. All the things I was worried about all along."

"But you couldn't have protected them from this. This is all their dad's fault."

"You and I might understand that but their dad has always been able to spin everything into being my fault. As he always tells me, he will always be able to lie better than I can tell the truth."

"That's sick."

"That's Ted in a nutshell." We paused again, both enjoying the crusty, gooey pizza with dollops of fresh burrata dotted across the top.

"Speaking of men in our lives," I changed the subject. "What's up with Jim? I've tried to give you space, but now I want all the details," I smiled, taking another bite.

Megan's face flushed, and she quickly took a bite of her slice.

"Well?" I pushed.

"He's a very kind man," said Megan without looking up and with her blush intensifying.

"And?" I pushed.

"And I like him very much," she added, continuing to study her plate.

I reached across and grabbed her hand, squeezing. "I'm so happy for you, Megan; you deserve it," I beamed.

"It's hard because I still love Bill. But Jim has been very understanding, and we're going slowly."

"Of course. Your love for Bill will never leave, but your heart is big enough for two loves. Jim is lucky to have you." Her blush renewed.

"I think Bill would be happy for me too. He told me at the end that he didn't want me to be alone. But having had a man like Bill, I didn't want to settle. So, it took me a while. Jim seems special. He makes me happy."

"And that makes me happy," I responded.

"And you? What's up with Finn? I know you were worried how he'd respond to everything with Ted and how you handled all of it," prodded Megan.

"He seems to have understood why I did what I did. He's kind, supportive, funny. I think I'm falling for him." Now, it was my turn to blush.

"Well, would you look at us!" exclaimed Megan. "Two women in our prime with some hot beaus!" I laughed, reveling in this new friendship I had found.

We finished our pizza, and then I walked Megan back to Grounded.

"Talk to you later, chica," she said with a wink as she sashayed into her shop.

I walked back home and texted MJ on the way, setting up to speak to her once I got home. I was barely through the door when my FaceTime rang, and MJ's name flashed across my phone screen. I pulled off my coat and flopped on the couch with Pumpkin, answering.

"Hey, MJ!"

"Hey yourself, Maggie. Spill the tea," she said, eagerly leaning into the camera.

I smiled and then took her through Ted's attack, the fall-out and finally, my conversation with Amber.

"Well butter my backside and call me a biscuit," she quipped, once I was done. "You're lucky to be alive. That son of a gun should spend the rest of his life in jail. Send him down here to us in Texas, we'll take care of him real good."

"Hold your horses, MJ. The justice system has him now. Between Connecticut, New York, and Texas he's out of my life for good, one way or another."

She smiled, breaking the seriousness of the conversation, saying "Hang on, you threatened Amber with Texas?"

I laughed, "Not really Texas as much as with her past."

We both laughed together and replayed the twists and turns of the case.

"I couldn't have done any of this without you, MJ; I don't know how to thank you."

"No thanks needed. It's what I do. Plus, anytime I can stick it to a bastard husband, I'm all for it. Anyway, you're the one who caught the link to the Brass Ass and followed the breadcrumbs. You're the one who stepped into the Supermax. That took balls."

"Thanks, MJ. Anytime you're in Connecticut you've got a friend and a place to stay. I'd love to thank you for your help in person."

"Same goes for you in Texas darlin', although I can see why it wouldn't be your first stop."

I chuckled and thanked her for the offer.

"Take good care now, ya' hear?"

"Will do, MJ, you too." We disconnected with a wave.

Pumpkin curled against me on the couch and I gingerly leaned over her, avoiding her stitches, to nuzzle into the soft fur behind her ears.

"It's just you and me again, girl. Thank you for protecting me and taking care of me." She harumphed in response as her eyes fluttered close into a nap.

"Good idea," I said and snuggled down next to her to sleep off the worry and stress of the past six months.

❖

Chapter 30 – Unwritten

Christmas night, Carter and I sat on the couch in front of the fire and the glow of the tree lights. We each sipped hot cocoa as carols played in the background.

"One of my favorite traditions," he said.

"You say that every year, but I agree," I smiled in response.

Meryl and Ruby joined us, wearing the matching Christmas pajamas that I had given them, each cradling a cup of cocoa with a candy cane hanging over the side. We all sat in silence, watching the fire jump and crack, and the tree lights flicker. I gazed at the Christmas cards hung along a string over the mantle. The card of honor was from Steve Croft. It included a picture of him and his now thirteen-year-old daughter. Once he was released from prison, he had written me an old fashioned, hand-written letter of thanks and this card was a terrific follow-up on his reunion with his daughter.

I couldn't help smiling at that outcome. The doorbell jolted me out of my thoughts. I pulled myself up and let Finn in to join us. He had gone into the station after Christmas supper to check on things and had promised to come back as soon as he could. Megan and Jim had also been with us to celebrate but had headed home when Finn went in to work.

"Hope I'm not interrupting family time," he said. "But I come bearing gifts." He lifted his fiddle case with a smile.

"Carter, freshen those cocoas, and let's get this party started," he said with a wink to me. Finn took a seat in the armchair next to the couch and, once settled, began to play. Glorious music flowed from his fiddle, and the girls each downloaded lyrics to classic Irish songs so we could all sing along.

Galway Girl, Molly Malone, and The Wild Rover were all favorites as the fiddle carried our spirits along to the melodies. Meryl sang duets with Finn, having the only clear voice in our family, and the rest of us couldn't keep ourselves from joining in the choruses. We had joked for years that only one Melody could carry a tune. When we tired of singing, Finn played haunting Irish ballads, which lulled both Ruby and Pumpkin to sleep.

Eventually, Carter and Meryl roused Ruby, and we all turned in after a long day. Finn stayed over with tacit understanding from my kids, and the two of us snuggled together under the heavy duvet against the cold night with Pumpkin curled at our feet.

"Merry Christmas, Mike. Thank you for making it all so special. You're wonderful on your fiddle; you've been holding out on me."

"And happy Christmas to you too, Maggie. Thank you for including me in your family today. I know this has been a hell of a year for you all."

"Yeah, it has. But I'm so proud of how my kids have handled it. They are each dealing with it differently and allowing each other the space for that."

"And you? How are you after the last year?"

"I'm good. It feels like I survived a very slow train wreck that was happening in my life. I feel really free for the first time in a long time."

I paused, nestled in the crook of his arm.

"There's a song that has always spoken to me. The lyrics say, 'Live your life with arms wide open, Today is where your book begins, the rest is still unwritten.' And I can't wait to see what my next chapter holds."

❖

About the Author

Laura Heeger is an attorney and former prosecutor in New York City. She lives in a small Connecticut village, practices global compliance, and lectures at the University of Connecticut Law School. She is happily married to Mike, and together they have four kids, now all grown, and a beloved French bulldog. She is passionate about writing, reading, gardening, and travel, and she loves a good mystery.

www.ingramcontent.com/pod-product-compliance
Lightning Source LLC
Chambersburg PA
CBHW022116310726
48972CB00007B/2069